Sarah Orne Jewett

Tales of New England

Sarah Orne Jewett

Tales of New England

ISBN/EAN: 9783337072339

Printed in Europe, USA, Canada, Australia, Japan

Cover: Foto ©Andreas Hilbeck / pixelio.de

More available books at **www.hansebooks.com**

TALES OF NEW ENGLAND

BY

SARAH ORNE JEWETT

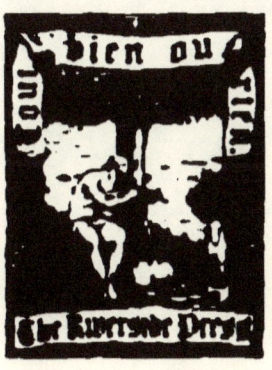

BOSTON AND NEW YORK

HOUGHTON, MIFFLIN AND COMPANY

The Riverside Press, Cambridge

1894

CONTENTS.

MISS TEMPY'S WATCHERS.

THE time of year was April; the place was a small farming town in New Hampshire, remote from any railroad. One by one the lights had been blown out in the scattered houses near Miss Tempy Dent's; but as her neighbors took a last look out-of-doors, their eyes turned with instinctive curiosity toward the old house, where a lamp burned steadily. They gave a little sigh. "Poor Miss Tempy!" said more than one bereft acquaintance; for the good woman lay dead in her north chamber, and the light was a watcher's light. The funeral was set for the next day, at one o'clock.

The watchers were two of the oldest friends, Mrs. Crowe and Sarah Ann Binson. They were sitting in the kitchen, because it seemed less awesome than the unused best room, and they beguiled the long hours by steady conversation. One would think that neither topics nor opinions would hold out, at that rate, all through the long spring night; but there was a certain degree of excitement just then, and the two women had risen to an unusual level of expressiveness and confidence. Each had already told the other more than one fact that she had determined to keep secret; they were again and again tempted into statements that either would have found impossible by daylight. Mrs. Crowe was knitting a blue yarn stocking for her husband; the foot was already so long that it seemed as if she must have forgotten to narrow it at the proper time. Mrs. Crowe knew exactly what she was about, however; she was of a much cooler disposition than Sister Binson, who made futile attempts at some sewing, only to drop her work into her lap whenever the talk was most engaging.

Their faces were interesting, — of the dry, shrewd, quick-witted New England type, with thin hair twisted neatly back out of the way. Mrs. Crowe could look vague and benignant, and Miss Binson was, to quote her neighbors, a little too sharp-set; but the world knew that she had need to be, with the load she must carry of supporting an ineffi-

cient widowed sister and six unpromising
and unwilling nieces and nephews. The eld-
est boy was at last placed with a good man
to learn the mason's trade. Sarah Ann Binson, for all her sharp, anxious aspect, never
defended herself, when her sister whined
and fretted. She was told every week of her
life that the poor children never would have
had to lift a finger if their father had lived,
and yet she had kept her steadfast way with
the little farm, and patiently taught the
young people many useful things, for which,
as everybody said, they would live to thank
her. However pleasureless her life appeared
to outward view, it was brimful of pleasure
to herself.

Mrs. Crowe, on the contrary, was well to
do, her husband being a rich farmer and an
easy-going man. She was a stingy woman,
but for all that she looked kindly; and when
she gave away anything, or lifted a finger to
help anybody, it was thought a great piece
of beneficence, and a compliment, indeed,
which the recipient accepted with twice as
much gratitude as double the gift that came
from a poorer and more generous acquaintance. Everybody liked to be on good terms
with Mrs. Crowe. Socially she stood much

higher than Sarah Ann Binson. They were both old schoolmates and friends of Temperance Dent, who had asked them, one day, not long before she died, if they would not come together and look after the house, and manage everything, when she was gone. She may have had some hope that they might become closer friends in this period of intimate partnership, and that the richer woman might better understand the burdens of the poorer. They had not kept the house the night before; they were too weary with the care of their old friend, whom they had not left until all was over.

There was a brook which ran down the hillside very near the house, and the sound of it was much louder than usual. When there was silence in the kitchen, the busy stream had a strange insistence in its wild voice, as if it tried to make the watchers understand something that related to the past.

"I declare, I can't begin to sorrow for Tempy yet. I am so glad to have her at rest," whispered Mrs. Crowe. "It is strange to set here without her, but I can't make it clear that she has gone. I feel as if she had got easy and dropped off to sleep, and I 'm more scared about waking her up than knowing any other feeling."

"Yes," said Sarah Ann, "it's just like that, ain't it? But I tell you we are goin' to miss her worse than we expect. She's helped me through with many a trial, has Temperance. I ain't the only one who says the same, neither."

These words were spoken as if there were a third person listening; somebody beside Mrs. Crowe. The watchers could not rid their minds of the feeling that they were being watched themselves. The spring wind whistled in the window crack, now and then, and buffeted the little house in a gusty way that had a sort of companionable effect. Yet, on the whole, it was a very still night, and the watchers spoke in a half-whisper.

"She was the freest-handed woman that ever I knew," said Mrs. Crowe, decidedly. "According to her means, she gave away more than anybody. I used to tell her 't wa'n't right. I used really to be afraid that she went without too much, for we have a duty to ourselves."

Sister Binson looked up in a half-amused, unconscious way, and then recollected herself.

Mrs. Crowe met her look with a serious face. "It ain't so easy for me to give as it

is for some," she said simply, but with an effort which was made possible only by the occasion. " I should like to say, while Tempy
is laying here yet in her own house, that she
has been a constant lesson to me. Folks are
too kind, and shame me with thanks for what
I do. I ain't such a generous woman as
poor Tempy was, for all she had nothin' to
do with, as one may say."

Sarah Binson was much moved at this
confession, and was even pained and touched
by the unexpected humility. " You have a
good many calls on you " — she began, and
then left her kind little compliment half finished.

" Yes, yes, but I 've got means enough.
My disposition 's more of a cross to me as
I grow older, and I made up my mind this
morning that Tempy's example should be
my pattern henceforth." She began to knit
faster than ever.

" 'T ain 't no use to get morbid : that 's
what Tempy used to say herself," said Sarah
Ann, after a minute's silence. " Ain't it
strange to say ' used to say ' ? " and her own
voice choked a little. " She never did like
to hear folks git goin' about themselves."

" 'T was only because they 're apt to do it

so as other folks will say 't was n't so, an'
praise 'em up," humbly replied Mrs. Crowe,
"and that ain't my object. There wa'n't a
child but what Tempy set herself to work
to see what she could do to please it. One
time my brother's folks had been stopping
here in the summer, from Massachusetts.
The children was all little, and they broke
up a sight of toys, and left 'em when they
were going away. Tempy come right up
after they rode by, to see if she could n't
help me set the house to rights, and she
caught me just as I was going to fling some
of the clutter into the stove. I was kind of
tired out, starting 'em off in season. 'Oh,
give me them!' says she, real pleading; and
she wropped 'em up and took 'em home with
her when she went, and she mended 'em up
and stuck 'em together, and made some young
one or other happy with every blessed one.
You 'd thought I 'd done her the biggest
favor. 'No thanks to me. I should ha'
burnt 'em, Tempy,' says I."

"Some of 'em came to our house, I
know," said Miss Binson. "She 'd take a
lot o' trouble to please a child, 'stead o'
shoving of it out o' the way, like the rest of
us when we 're drove."

" I can tell you the biggest thing she ever
done, and I don't know 's there 's anybody
left but me to tell it.　I don't want it forgot," Sarah Binson went on, looking up at
the clock to see how the night was going.
" It was that pretty-looking Trevor girl, who
taught the Corners school, and married so
well afterwards, out in New York State.
You remember her, I dare say ? "

" Certain," said Mrs. Crowe, with an air
of interest.

" She was a splendid scholar, folks said,
and give the school a great start ; but she 'd
overdone herself getting her education, and
working to pay for it, and she all broke
down one spring, and Tempy made her
come and stop with her a while, — you remember that ?　Well, she had an uncle, her
mother's brother, out in Chicago, who was
well off and friendly, and used to write to
Lizzie Trevor, and I dare say make her
some presents ; but he was a lively, driving
man, and did n't take time to stop and think
about his folks.　He had n't seen her since
she was a little girl.　Poor Lizzie was so
pale and weakly that she just got through the
term o' school.　She looked as if she was just
going straight off in a decline.　Tempy, she

cosseted her up a while, and then, next thing
folks knew, she was tellin' round how Miss
Trevor had gone to see her uncle, and meant
to visit Niagary Falls on the way, and stop
over night. Now I happened to know, in
ways I won't dwell on to explain, that the
poor girl was in debt for her schoolin' when
she come here, and her last quarter's pay
had just squared it off at last, and left her
without a cent ahead, hardly ; but it had
fretted her thinking of it, so she paid it all ;
those might have dunned her that she owed
it to. An' I taxed Tempy about the girl's
goin' off on such a journey till she owned
up, rather 'n have Lizzie blamed, that she 'd
given her sixty dollars, same 's if she was
rolling in riches, and sent her off to have a
good rest and vacation."

"Sixty dollars ! " exclaimed Mrs. Crowe.
"Tempy only had ninety dollars a year that
came in to her ; rest of her livin' she got by
helpin' about, with what she raised off this
little piece o' ground, sand one side an' clay
the other. An' how often I 've heard her
tell, years ago, that she 'd rather see Niagary
than any other sight in the world ! "

The women looked at each other in silence ; the magnitude of the generous sacri-

fice was almost too great for their compre-
hension.

" She was just poor enough to do that ! "
declared Mrs. Crowe at last, in an abandon-
ment of feeling. " Say what you may, I
feel humbled to the dust," and her companion ventured to say nothing. She never had
given away sixty dollars at once, but it was
simply because she never had it to give. It
came to her very lips to say in explanation,
"Tempy was so situated ; " but she checked
herself in time, for she would not betray
her own loyal guarding of a dependent
household.

" Folks say a great deal of generosity,
and this one's being public-sperited, and
that one free-handed about giving," said
Mrs. Crowe, who was a little nervous in the
silence. " I suppose we can't tell the sorrow it would be to some folks not to give,
same 's 't would be to me not to save. I
seem kind of made for that, as if 't was what
I 'd got to do. I should feel sights better
about it if I could make it evident what I
was savin' for. If I had a child, now, Sarah Ann," and her voice was a little husky,
— " if I had a child, I should think I was
heapin' of it up because he was the one

trained by the Lord to scatter it again for good. But here's Mr. Crowe and me, we can't do anything with money, and both of us like to keep things same's they've always been. Now Priscilla Dance was talking away like a mill-clapper, week before last. She'd think I would go right off and get one o' them new-fashioned gilt-and-white papers for the best room, and some new furniture, an' a marble-top table. And I looked at her, all struck up. 'Why,' says I, 'Priscilla, that nice old velvet paper ain't hurt a mite. I shouldn't feel 't was my best room without it. Dan'el says 't is the first thing he can remember rubbin' his little baby fingers on to it, and how splendid he thought them red roses was.' I maintain," continued Mrs. Crowe stoutly, "that folks wastes sights o' good money doin' just such foolish things. Tearin' out the insides o' meetin'-houses, and fixin' the pews different; 't was good enough as 't was with mendin'; then times come, an' they want to put it all back same's 't was before."

This touched upon an exciting subject to active members of that parish. Miss Binson and Mrs. Crowe belonged to opposite parties, and had at one time come as near hard

feelings as they could, and yet escape them.
Each hastened to speak of other things and
to show her untouched friendliness.

"I do agree with you," said Sister Binson,
"that few of us know what use to make
of money, beyond every - day necessities.
You 've seen more o' the world than I have,
and know what 's expected. When it comes
to taste and judgment about such things, I
ought to defer to others; " and with this
modest avowal the critical moment passed
when there might have been an improper
discussion.

In the silence that followed, the fact of
their presence in a house of death grew more
clear than before. There was something
disturbing in the noise of a mouse gnawing
at the dry boards of a closet wall near by.
Both the watchers looked up anxiously at
the clock; it was almost the middle of the
night, and the whole world seemed to have
left them alone with their solemn duty.
Only the brook was awake.

"Perhaps we might give a look up-stairs
now," whispered Mrs. Crowe, as if she
hoped to hear some reason against their going just then to the chamber of death; but
Sister Binson rose, with a serious and yet

satisfied countenance, and lifted the small lamp from the table. She was much more used to watching than Mrs. Crowe, and much less affected by it. They opened the door into a small entry with a steep stairway; they climbed the creaking stairs, and entered the cold upper room on tiptoe. Mrs. Crowe's heart began to beat very fast as the lamp was put on a high bureau, and made long, fixed shadows about the walls. She went hesitatingly toward the solemn shape under its white drapery, and felt a sense of remonstrance as Sarah Ann gently, but in a business-like way, turned back the thin sheet.

"Seems to me she looks pleasanter and pleasanter," whispered Sarah Ann Binson impulsively, as they gazed at the white face with its wonderful smile. "To-morrow 't will all have faded out. I do believe they kind of wake up a day or two after they die, and it 's then they go." She replaced the light covering, and they both turned quickly away; there was a chill in this upper room.

"'T is a great thing for anybody to have got through, ain't it?" said Mrs. Crowe softly, as she began to go down the stairs on tiptoe. The warm air from the kitchen beneath met them with a sense of welcome and shelter.

"I don' know why it is, but I feel as near again to Tempy down here as I do up there," replied Sister Binson. "I feel as if the air was full of her, kind of. I can sense things, now and then, that she seems to say. Now I never was one to take up with no nonsense of sperits and such, but I declare I felt as if she told me just now to put some more wood into the stove."

Mrs. Crowe preserved a gloomy silence. She had suspected before this that her companion was of a weaker and more credulous disposition than herself. "'T is a great thing to have got through," she repeated, ignoring definitely all that had last been said. "I suppose you know as well as I that Tempy was one that always feared death. Well, it 's all put behind her now; she knows what 't is." Mrs. Crowe gave a little sigh, and Sister Binson's quick sympathies were stirred toward this other old friend, who also dreaded the great change.

"I 'd never like to forgit almost those last words Tempy spoke plain to me," she said gently, like the comforter she truly was. "She looked up at me once or twice, that

last afternoon after I come to set by her, and
let Mis' Owen go home; and I says, 'Can I
do anything to ease you, Tempy?' and the
tears come into my eyes so I could n't see
what kind of a nod she give me. 'No, Sarah
Ann, you can't, dear,' says she; and then
she got her breath again, and says she, looking at me real meanin', 'I 'm only a-gettin'
sleepier and sleepier; that's all there is,'
says she, and smiled up at me kind of wish-
ful, and shut her eyes. I knew well enough
all she meant. She 'd been lookin' out for
a chance to tell me, and I don' know's she
ever said much afterwards."

Mrs. Crowe was not knitting; she had
been listening too eagerly. "Yes, 't will be
a comfort to think of that sometimes," she
said, in acknowledgment.

"I know that old Dr. Prince said once,
in evenin' meetin', that he 'd watched by
many a dyin' bed, as we well knew, and
enough o' his sick folks had been scared o'
dyin' their whole lives through; but when
they come to the last, he 'd never seen one
but was willin', and most were glad, to go.
' 'T is as natural as bein' born or livin' on,'
he said. I don't know what had moved him
to speak that night. You know he wa'n't

in the habit of it, and 't was the monthly
concert of prayer for foreign missions anyways," said Sarah Ann; " but 't was a great
stay to the mind to listen to his words of experience."

" There never was a better man," responded Mrs. Crowe, in a really cheerful
tone. She had recovered from her feeling
of nervous dread, the kitchen was so comfortable with lamplight and firelight; and
just then the old clock began to tell the hour
of twelve with leisurely whirring strokes.

Sister Binson laid aside her work, and
rose quickly and went to the cupboard.
"We'd better take a little to eat," she explained. " The night will go fast after this.
I want to know if you went and made some
o' your nice cupcake, while you was home
to-day?" she asked, in a pleased tone; and
Mrs. Crowe acknowledged such a gratify-
ing piece of thoughtfulness for this humble
friend who denied herself all luxuries.
Sarah Ann brewed a generous cup of tea,
and the watchers drew their chairs up to
the table presently, and quelled their hun-
ger with good country appetites. Sister Binson put a spoon into a small, old-fashioned
glass of preserved quince, and passed it to

her friend. She was most familiar with the house, and played the part of hostess. "Spread some o' this on your bread and butter," she said to Mrs. Crowe. "Tempy wanted me to use some three or four times, but I never felt to. I know she'd like to have us comfortable now, and would urge us to make a good supper, poor dear."

"What excellent preserves she did make!" mourned Mrs. Crowe. "None of us has got her light hand at doin' things tasty. She made the most o' everything, too. Now, she only had that one old quince-tree down in the far corner of the piece, but she'd go out in the spring and tend to it, and look at it so pleasant, and kind of expect the old thorny thing into bloomin'."

"She was just the same with folks," said Sarah Ann. "And she'd never git more 'n a little apernful o' quinces, but she'd have every mite o' goodness out o' those, and set the glasses up onto her best-room closet shelf, so pleased. 'T wa'n't but a week ago to-morrow mornin' I fetched her a little taste o' jelly in a teaspoon ; and she says 'Thank ye,' and took it, an' the minute she tasted it she looked up at me as worried as could be. 'Oh, I don't want to eat that,' says she.

'I always keep that in case o' sickness.'
'You're goin' to have the good o' one tumbler
yourself,' says I. 'I'd just like to know
who's sick now, if you ain't!' An' she
could n't help laughin', I spoke up so smart.
Oh, dear me, how I shall miss talkin' over
things with her! She always sensed things,
and got just the p'int you meant."

"She did n't begin to age until two or
three years ago, did she?" asked Mrs.
Crowe. "I never saw anybody keep her
looks as Tempy did. She looked young long
after I begun to feel like an old woman.
The doctor used to say 't was her young
heart, and I don't know but what he was
right. How she did do for other folks!
There was one spell she was n't at home a
day to a fortnight. She got most of her
livin' so, and that made her own potatoes
and things last her through. None o' the
young folks could get married without her,
and all the old ones was disappointed if she
wa'n't round when they was down with
sickness and had to go. An' cleanin', or
tailorin' for boys, or rug-hookin', — there
was nothin' but what she could do as handy
as most. 'I do love to work,' — ain't you
heard her say that twenty times a week?"

Sarah Ann Binson nodded, and began to clear away the empty plates. "We may want a taste o' somethin' more towards mornin'," she said. "There's plenty in the closet here; and in case some comes from a distance to the funeral, we'll have a little table spread after we get back to the house."

"Yes, I was busy all the mornin'. I've cooked up a sight o' things to bring over," said Mrs. Crowe. "I felt 't was the last I could do for her."

They drew their chairs near the stove again, and took up their work. Sister Binson's rocking-chair creaked as she rocked; the brook sounded louder than ever. It was more lonely when nobody spoke, and presently Mrs. Crowe returned to her thoughts of growing old.

"Yes, Tempy aged all of a sudden. I remember I asked her if she felt as well as common, one day, and she laughed at me good. There, when Mr. Crowe begun to look old, I could n't help feeling as if somethin' ailed him, and like as not 't was somethin' he was goin' to git right over, and I dosed him for it stiddy, half of one summer."

"How many things we shall be wanting to ask Tempy!" exclaimed Sarah Ann

Binson, after a long pause. " I can't make up my mind to doin' without her. I wish folks could come back just once, and tell us how 'tis where they 've gone. Seems then we could do without 'em better."

The brook hurried on, the wind blew about the house now and then; the house itself was a silent place, and the supper, the warm fire, and an absence of any new topics for conversation made the watchers drowsy. Sister Binson closed her eyes first, to rest them for a minute; and Mrs. Crowe glanced at her compassionately, with a new sympathy for the hard-worked little woman. She made up her mind to let Sarah Ann have a good rest, while she kept watch alone; but in a few minutes her own knitting was dropped, and she, too, fell asleep. Overhead, the pale shape of Tempy Dent, the outworn body of that generous, loving-hearted, simple soul, slept on also in its white raiment. Perhaps Tempy herself stood near, and saw her own life and its surroundings with new understanding. Perhaps she herself was the only watcher.

Later, by some hours, Sarah Ann Binson woke with a start. There was a pale light of dawn outside the small windows. Inside the kitchen, the lamp burned dim. Mrs. Crowe awoke, too.

"I think Tempy'd be the first to say 't was just as well we both had some rest," she said, not without a guilty feeling.

Her companion went to the outer door, and opened it wide. The fresh air was none too cold, and the brook's voice was not nearly so loud as it had been in the midnight darkness. She could see the shapes of the hills, and the great shadows that lay across the lower country. The east was fast growing bright.

"'T will be a beautiful day for the funeral," she said, and turned again, with a sigh, to follow Mrs. Crowe up the stairs.

THE DULHAM LADIES.

To be leaders of society in the town of Dulham was as satisfactory to Miss Dobin and Miss Lucinda Dobin as if Dulham were London itself. Of late years, though they would not allow themselves to suspect such treason, the most ill-bred of the younger people in the village made fun of them behind their backs, and laughed at their treasured summer mantillas, their mincing steps, and the shape of their parasols.

They were always conscious of the fact that they were the daughters of a once eminent Dulham minister; but beside this unanswerable claim to the respect of the First Parish, they were aware that their mother's social position was one of superior altitude. Madam Dobin's grandmother was a Greenaple of Boston. In her younger days she had often visited her relatives, the Greenaples and Hightrees, and in seasons of festivity she could relate to a select and properly

excited audience her delightful experiences
of town life. Nothing could be finer than
her account of having taken tea at Governor
Clovenfoot's, on Beacon Street, in company
with an English lord, who was indulging
himself in a brief vacation from his arduous
duties at the Court of St. James.

"He exclaimed that he had seldom seen
in England so beautiful and intelligent a
company of ladies," Madam Dobin would
always say in conclusion. "He was deco-
rated with the blue ribbon of the Knights
of the Garter." Miss Dobin and Miss Lucinda thought for many years that this famous blue ribbon was tied about the noble
gentleman's leg. One day they even discussed the question openly; Miss Dobin
placing the decoration at his knee, and Miss
Lucinda locating it much lower down, according to the length of the short gray socks
with which she was familiar.

"You have no imagination, Lucinda,"
the elder sister replied impatiently. "Of
course, those were the days of small-clothes
and long silk stockings!" — whereat Miss
Lucinda was rebuked, but not persuaded.

"I wish that my dear girls could have
the outlook upon society which fell to my

portion," Madam Dobin sighed, after she
had set these ignorant minds to rights, and
enriched them by communicating the final
truth about the blue ribbon. " I must not
chide you for the absence of opportunities,
but if our cousin Harriet Greenaple were
only living, you would not lack enjoyment
or social education."

Madam Dobin had now been dead a great
many years. She seemed an elderly woman
to her daughters some time before she left
them ; they thought later that she had really
died comparatively young, since their own
years had come to equal the record of hers.
When they visited her tall white tombstone
in the orderly Dulham burying-ground, it
was a strange thought to both the daughters
that they were older women than their mother
had been when she died. To be sure, it was
the fashion to appear older in her day, —
they could remember the sober effect of
really youthful married persons in cap and
frisette ; but, whether they owed it to the
changed times or to their own qualities, they
felt no older themselves than ever they had.
Beside upholding the ministerial dignity of
their father, they were obliged to give a

lenient sanction to the ways of the world
for their mother's sake; and they combined
the two duties with reverence and impartial-
ity.

Madam Dobin was, in her prime, a walking example of refinement and courtesy. If
she erred in any way, it was by keeping too
strict watch and rule over her small king-
dom. She acted with great dignity in all
matters of social administration and etiquette, but, while it must be owned that the
parishioners felt a sense of freedom for a
time after her death, in their later years
they praised and valued her more and more,
and often lamented her generously and sin-
cerely.

Several of her distinguished relatives attended Madam Dobin's funeral, which was
long considered the most dignified and elegant pageant of that sort which had ever
taken place in Dulham. It seemed to mark
the close of a famous epoch in Dulham history, and it was increasingly difficult forever
afterward to keep the tone of society up to
the old standard. Somehow, the distinguished relatives had one by one disappeared, though they all had excellent rea-
sons for the discontinuance of their visits.

A few had left this world altogether, and
the family circle of the Greenaples and
Hightrees was greatly reduced in circumfer-
ence. Sometimes, in summer, a stray connection drifted Dulham-ward, and was displayed to the townspeople (not to say
paraded) by the gratified hostesses. It was
a disappointment if the guest could not be
persuaded to remain over Sunday and appear at church. When household antiqui-
ties became fashionable, the ladies remarked
upon a surprising interest in their corner
cupboard and best chairs, and some distant
relatives revived their almost forgotten custom of paying a summer visit to Dulham.
They were not long in finding out with
what desperate affection Miss Dobin and
Miss Lucinda clung to their mother's wedding china and other inheritances, and were
allowed to depart without a single teacup.
One graceless descendant of the Hightrees
prowled from garret to cellar, and admired
the household belongings diligently, but she
was not asked to accept even the dislocated
cherry-wood footstool that she had discovered in the far corner of the parsonage pew.

Some of the Dulham friends had always
suspected that Madam Dobin made a social

misstep when she chose the Reverend Edward Dobin for her husband. She was no longer young when she married, and though she had gone through the wood and picked up a crooked stick at last, it made a great difference that her stick possessed an ecclesiastical bark. · The Reverend Edward was, moreover, a respectable graduate of Harvard College, and to a woman of her standards a clergyman was by no means insignificant. It was impossible not to respect his office, at any rate, and she must have treated him with proper veneration for the sake of that, if for no other reason, though his early advantages had been insufficient, and he was quite insensible to the claims of the Greenaple pedigree, and preferred an Indian pudding to pie crust that was, without exaggeration, half a quarter high. The delicacy of Madam Dobin's touch and preference in everything, from hymns to cookery, was quite lost upon this respected preacher, yet he was not without pride or complete confidence in his own decisions.

The Reverend Mr. Dobin was never very enlightening in his discourses, and was providentially stopped short by a stroke of paralysis in the middle of his clerical career. He

lived on and on through many dreary years,
but his children never accepted the fact that
he was a tyrant, and served him humbly and
patiently. He fell at last into a condition
of great incapacity and chronic trembling,
but was able for nearly a quarter of a century to be carried to the meeting-house from
time to time to pronounce farewell discourses. On high days of the church he
was always placed in the pulpit, and held
up his shaking hands when the benediction
was pronounced, as if the divine gift were
exclusively his own, and the other minister
did but say empty words. Afterward he
was usually tired and displeased and hard
to cope with, but there was always a proper
notice taken of these too often recurring
events. For old times' and for pity's sake
and from natural goodness of heart, the
elder parishioners rallied manfully about
the Reverend Mr. Dobin ; and whoever his
successor or colleague might be, the Dobins
were always called the minister's folks, while
the active laborer in that vineyard was only
Mr. Smith or Mr. Jones, as the case might
be. At last the poor old man died, to
everybody's relief and astonishment ; and
after he was properly preached about and

lamented, his daughters, Miss Dobin and
Miss Lucinda, took a good look at life from
a new standpoint, and decided that, now they
were no longer constrained by home duties,
they must make themselves of a great deal
more use to the town.

Sometimes there is such a household as
this (which has been perhaps too minutely
described), where the parents linger until
their children are far past middle age, and always keep them in a too childish and unworthy state of subjection. The Misses Dobin's
characters were much influenced by such an
unnatural prolongation of the filial relation-
ship, and they were amazingly slow to suspect
that they were not so young as they used to
be. There was nothing to measure themselves by but Dulham people and things.
The elm-trees were growing yet, and many
of the ladies of the First Parish were older
than they, and called them, with pleasant
familiarity, the Dobin girls. These elderly
persons seemed really to be growing old,
and Miss Lucinda frequently lamented the
change in society; she thought it a freak of
nature and too sudden blighting of earthly
hopes that several charming old friends of
her mother's were no longer living. They

were advanced in age when Miss Lucinda
was a young girl, though time and space are
but relative, after all.

Their influence upon society would have
made a great difference in many ways. Certainly, the new parishioners, who had often
enough been instructed to pronounce their
pastor's name as if it were spelled with one
" b," would not have boldly returned again
and again to their obnoxious habit of saying
Dobbin. Miss Lucinda might carefully
speak to the neighbor and new-comers of
" my sister, Miss Do-bin ; " only the select
company of intimates followed her lead, and
at last there was something humiliating
about it, even though many persons spoke
of them only as " the ladies."

" The name was originally *D'Aubigne*,
we think," Miss Lucinda would say coldly
and patiently, as if she had already explained this foolish mistake a thousand
times too often. It was like the sorrows in
many a provincial château in the Reign of
Terror. The ladies looked on with increasing dismay at the retrogression in society.
They felt as if they were a feeble garrison, to whose lot it had fallen to repulse a
noisy, irreverent mob, an increasing band of

marauders who would overthrow all land-
marks of the past, all etiquette and social
rank. The new minister himself was a
round-faced, unspiritual-looking young man,
whom they would have instinctively ignored
if he had not been a minister. The new
people who came to Dulham were not like
the older residents, and they had no desire
to be taught better. Little they cared about
the Greenaples or the Hightrees; and once,
when Miss Dobin essayed to speak of some
detail of her mother's brilliant experiences
in Boston high life, she was interrupted, and
the new-comer who sat next her at the parish
sewing society began to talk about something
else. We cannot believe that it could have
been the tea-party at Governor Clovenfoot's
which the rude creature so disrespectfully
ignored, but some persons are capable of
showing any lack of good taste.

The ladies had an unusual and most pain-
ful sense of failure, as they went home together that evening. " I have always made
it my object to improve and interest the
people at such times; it would seem so possible to elevate their thoughts and direct
them into higher channels," said Miss Dobin
sadly. " But as for that Woolden woman,

there is no use in casting pearls before
swine ! "

Miss Lucinda murmured an indignant as-
sent. She had a secret suspicion that the
Woolden woman had heard the story in
question oftener than had pleased her. She
was but an ignorant creature ; though she
had lived in Dulham twelve or thirteen
years, she was no better than when she
came. The mistake was in treating sister
Harriet as if she were on a level with the
rest of the company. Miss Lucinda had observed more than once, lately, that her sister
sometimes repeated herself, unconsciously, a
little oftener than was agreeable. Perhaps
they were getting a trifle dull; towards
spring it might be well to pass a few days
with some of their friends, and have a
change.

" If I have tried to do anything," said
Miss Dobin in an icy tone, " it has been to
stand firm in my lot and place, and to hold
the standard of cultivated mind and elegant
manners as high as possible. You would
think it had been a hundred years since our
mother's death, so completely has the effect
of her good breeding and exquisite hospitality been lost sight of, here in Dulham. I

could wish that our father had chosen to set-
tle in a larger and more appreciative place.
They would like to put us on the shelf, too.
I can see that plainly."

"I am sure we have our friends," said
Miss Lucinda anxiously, but with a choking
voice. "We must not let them think we do
not mean to keep up with the times, as we
always have. I do feel as if perhaps — our
hair " —

And the sad secret was out at last. Each
of the sisters drew a long breath of relief
at this beginning of a confession.

It was certain that they must take some
steps to retrieve their lost ascendency. Public attention had that evening been called to
their fast-disappearing locks, poor ladies;
and Miss Lucinda felt the discomfort most,
for she had been the inheritor of the High-
tree hair, long and curly, and chestnut in
color. There used to be a waviness about
it, and sometimes pretty escaping curls, but
these were gone long ago. Miss Dobin re-
sembled her father, and her hair had not
been luxuriant, so that she was less changed
by its absence than one might suppose. The
straightness and thinness had increased so
gradually that neither sister had quite ac-

cepted the thought that other persons would particularly notice their altered appearance.

They had shrunk, with the reticence born of close family association, from speaking of the cause even to each other, when they made themselves pretty little lace and dotted muslin caps. Breakfast caps, they called them, and explained that these were universally worn in town; the young Princess of Wales originated them, or at any rate adopted them. The ladies offered no apology for keeping the breakfast caps on until bedtime, and in spite of them a forward child had just spoken, loud and shrill, an untimely question in the ears of the for once silent sewing society. "Do Miss Dobbinses wear them great caps because their heads is cold?" the little beast had said; and everybody was startled and dismayed.

Miss Dobin had never shown better her good breeding and valor, the younger sister thought.

"No, little girl," replied the stately Harriet, with a chilly smile. "I believe that our headdresses are quite in the fashion for ladies of all ages. And you must remember that it is never polite to make such personal remarks." It was after this that Miss Do-

bin had been reminded of Madam Somebody's unusual headgear at the evening entertainment in Boston. Nobody but the
Woolden woman could have interrupted her
under such trying circumstances.

Miss Lucinda, however, was certain that
the time had come for making some effort
to replace her lost adornment. The child
had told an unwelcome truth, but had paved
the way for further action, and now was the
time to suggest something that had slowly
been taking shape in Miss Lucinda's mind.
A young grand-nephew of their mother and
his bride had passed a few days with them,
two or three summers before, and the sisters
had been quite shocked to find that the
pretty young woman wore a row of frizzes,
not originally her own, over her smooth
forehead. At the time, Miss Dobin and
Miss Lucinda had spoken severely with each
other of such bad taste, but now it made a
great difference that the wearer of the
frizzes was not only a relative by marriage
and used to good society, but also that she
came from town, and might be supposed to
know what was proper in the way of toilet.

" I really think, sister, that we had better
see about having some — arrangements, next

time we go anywhere," Miss Dobin said
unexpectedly, with a slight tremble in her
voice, just as they reached their own door.
" There seems to be quite a fashion for them
nowadays. For the parish's sake we ought
to recognize " — and Miss Lucinda responded with instant satisfaction. She did
not like to complain, but she had been
troubled with neuralgic pains in her forehead on suddenly meeting the cold air. The
sisters felt a new bond of sympathy in keeping this secret with and for each other ; they
took pains to say to several acquaintances
that they were thinking of going to the next
large town to do a few errands for Christmas.

A bright, sunny morning seemed to wish
the ladies good-fortune. Old Hetty Downs,
their faithful maid-servant and protector,
looked after them in affectionate foreboding. "Dear sakes, what devil's wiles may
be played on them blessed innocents afore
they're safe home again!" she murmured,
as they vanished round the corner of the
street that led to the railway station.

Miss Dobin and Miss Lucinda paced discreetly side by side down the main street of
Westbury. It was nothing like Boston, of
course, but the noise was slightly confusing,

and the passers-by sometimes roughly pushed
against them. Westbury was a consequen-
tial manufacturing town, but a great con-
venience at times like this. The trifling
Christmas gifts for their old neighbors and
Sunday-school scholars were purchased and
stowed away in their neat Fayal basket before the serious commission of the day was
attended to. Here and there, in the shops,
disreputable frizzes were displayed in un-
blushing effrontery, but no such vulgar
shopkeeper merited the patronage of the
Misses Dobin. They pretended not to observe the unattractive goods, and went their
way to a low, one-storied building on a side
street, where an old tradesman lived. He
had been useful to the minister while he still
remained upon the earth and had need of a
wig, sandy in hue and increasingly sprinkled
with gray, as if it kept pace with other
changes of existence. But old Paley's shut-
ters were up, and a bar of rough wood was
nailed firmly across the one that had lost its
fastening and would rack its feeble hinges
in the wind. Old Paley had always been
polite and bland; they really had looked
forward to a little chat with him; they had
heard a year or two before of his wife's

death, and meant to offer sympathy. His
business of hair-dressing had been carried
on with that of parasol and umbrella mending, and the condemned umbrella which was
his sign flapped and swung in the rising
wind, a tattered skeleton before the closed
door. The ladies sighed and turned away;
they were beginning to feel tired; the day
was long, and they had not met with any
pleasures yet. "We might walk up the
street a little farther," suggested Miss Lucinda; "that is, if you are not tired," as
they stood hesitating on the corner after
they had finished a short discussion of Mr.
Paley's disappearance. Happily it was only
a few minutes before they came to a stop
together in front of a new, shining shop,
where smirking waxen heads all in a row
were decked with the latest fashions of wigs
and frizzes. One smiling fragment of a
gentleman stared so straight at Miss Lucinda with his black eyes that she felt quite
coy and embarrassed, and was obliged to
feign not to be conscious of his admiration.
But Miss Dobin, after a brief delay, boldly
opened the door and entered; it was better
to be sheltered in the shop than exposed to
public remark as they gazed in at the win-

dows. Miss Lucinda felt her heart beat and her courage give out; she, coward like, left the transaction of their business to her sister, and turned to contemplate the back of the handsome model. It was a slight shock to find that he was not so attractive from this point of view. The wig he wore was well made all round, but his shoulders were roughly finished in a substance that looked like plain plaster of Paris.

"What can I have ze pleasure of showing you, young ladees?" asked a person who advanced; and Miss Lucinda faced about to discover a smiling, middle-aged Frenchman, who rubbed his hands together and looked at his customers, first one and then the other, with delightful deference. He seemed a very civil nice person, the young ladies thought.

"My sister and I were thinking of buying some little arrangements to wear above the forehead." Miss Dobin explained, with pathetic dignity; but the Frenchman spared her any further words. He looked with eager interest at the bonnets, as if no lack had attracted his notice before. "Ah, yes. *Je comprends;* ze high foreheads are not now ze mode. Je prefer them, moi, yes,

yes, but ze ladees must accept ze fashion;
zay must now cover ze forehead with ze
frizzes, ze bangs, you say. As you wis', as
you wis'!" and the tactful little man, with
many shrugs and merry gestures at such
girlish fancies, pulled down one box after
another.

It was a great relief to find that this was
no worse, to say the least, than any other
shopping, though the solemnity and secrecy
of the occasion were infringed upon by the
great supply of "arrangements" and the
loud discussion of the color of some crimps
a noisy girl was buying from a young sales-
woman the other side of the shop.

Miss Dobin waved aside the wares which
were being displayed for her approval.
"Something — more simple, if you please,"
— she did not like to say "older."

"But these are *très simple*," protested the
Frenchman. "We have nothing younger;"
and Miss Dobin and Miss Lucinda blushed,
and said no more. The Frenchman had his
own way; he persuaded them that nothing
was so suitable as some conspicuous fore-
locks that matched their hair as it used to
be. They would have given anything rather
than leave their breakfast caps at home, if

they had known that their proper winter bonnets must come off. They hardly listened to the wig merchant's glib voice as Miss Dobin stood revealed before the merciless mirror at the back of the shop.

He made everything as easy as possible, the friendly creature, and the ladies were grateful to him. Besides, now that the bonnet was on again there was a great improvement in Miss Dobin's appearance. She turned to Miss Lucinda, and saw a gleam of delight in her eager countenance. " It really is very becoming. I like the way it parts over your forehead," said the younger sister, " but if it were long enough to go behind the ears " — " *Non, non*," entreated the Frenchman. " To make her the old woman at once would be cruelty ! " And Lucinda, who was wondering how well she would look in her turn, succumbed promptly to such protestations. Yes, there was no use in being old before their time. Dulham was not quite keeping pace with the rest of the world in these days, but they need not drag behind everybody else, just because they lived there.

The price of the little arrangements was much less than the sisters expected, and the

uncomfortable expense of their reverend father's wigs had been, it was proved, a thing
of the past.   Miss Dobin treated her polite
Frenchman with great courtesy; indeed,
Miss Lucinda had more than once whispered to her to talk French, and as they were
bowed out of the shop the gracious *Bony-
sure* of the elder lady seemed to act like the
string of a showerbath, and bring down an
awesome torrent of foreign phrases upon
the two guileless heads.   It was impossible
to reply; the ladies bowed again, however,
and Miss Lucinda caught a last smile from
the handsome wax countenance in the window.   He appeared to regard her with fresh
approval, and she departed down the street
with mincing steps.

"I feel as if anybody might look at me
now, sister," said gentle Miss Lucinda.
"I confess, I have really suffered sometimes, since I knew I looked so distressed."

"Yours is lighter than I thought it was
in the shop," remarked Miss Dobin doubtfully, but she quickly added that perhaps
it would change a little.   She was so perfectly satisfied with her own appearance
that she could not bear to dim the pleasure
of any one else.   The truth remained that

she never would have let Lucinda choose
that particular arrangement if she had seen
it first in a good light. And Lucinda was
thinking exactly the same of her companion.

"I am sure we shall have no more neural-
gia," said Miss Dobin. "I am sorry we
waited so long, dear," and they tripped
down the main street of Westbury, confident that nobody would suspect them of
being over thirty. Indeed, they felt quite
girlish, and unconsciously looked sideways
as they went along, to see their satisfying
reflections in the windows. The great
panes made excellent mirrors, with not too
clear or lasting pictures of these comforted
passers-by.

The Frenchman in the shop was making
merry with his assistants. The two great
frisettes had long been out of fashion; he
had been lying in wait with them for two
unsuspecting country ladies, who could be
cajoled into such a purchase.

"Sister," Miss Lucinda was saying, "you
know there is still an hour to wait before
our train goes. Suppose we take a little
longer walk down the other side of the
way;" and they strolled slowly back again.

In fact, they nearly missed the train, naughty girls! Hetty would have been so worried, they assured each other, but they reached the station just in time.

"Lutie," said Miss Dobin, "put up your hand and part it from your forehead; it seems to be getting a little out of place;" and Miss Lucinda, who had just got breath enough to speak, returned the information that Miss Dobin's was almost covering her eyebrows. They might have to trim them a little shorter; of course it could be done. The darkness was falling; they had taken an early dinner before they started, and now they were tired and hungry after the exertion of the afternoon, but the spirit of youth flamed afresh in their hearts, and they were very happy. If one's heart remains young, it is a sore trial to have the outward appearance entirely at variance. It was the ladies' nature to be girlish, and they found it impossible not to be grateful to the flimsy, ineffectual disguise which seemed to set them right with the world. The old conductor, who had known them for many years, looked hard at them as he took their tickets, and, being a man of humor and compassion, affected not to notice

anything remarkable in their appearance.
" You ladies never mean to grow old, like
the rest of us," he said gallantly, and the
sisters fairly quaked with joy. Their young
hearts would forever keep them truly unconscious of the cruel thievery of time.

" Bless us ! " the obnoxious Mrs. Woolden
was saying, at the other end of the car.
" There's the old maid Dobbinses, and
they've bought 'em some bangs. I expect
they wanted to get thatched in a little before
real cold weather; but don't they look just
like a pair o' poodle dogs."

The little ladies descended wearily from
the train. Somehow they did not enjoy a
day's shopping as much as they used. They
were certainly much obliged to Hetty for
sending her niece's boy to meet them, with a
lantern ; also for having a good warm supper
ready when they came in. Hetty took a
quick look at her mistresses, and returned to
the kitchen. " I knew somebody would be
foolin' of 'em," she assured herself angrily,
but she had to laugh. Their dear, kind
faces were wrinkled and pale, and the great
frizzes had lost their pretty curliness, and
were hanging down, almost straight and very
ugly, into the ladies' eyes. They could not

tuck them up under their caps, as they were
sure might be done.

Then came a succession of rainy days,
and nobody visited the rejuvenated household. The frisettes looked very bright chestnut by the light of day, and it must be confessed that Miss Dobin took the scissors and
shortened Miss Lucinda's half an inch, and
Miss Lucinda returned the compliment quite
secretly, because each thought her sister's
forehead lower than her own. Their dear
gray eyebrows were honestly displayed, as if
it were the fashion not to have them match
with wigs. Hetty at last spoke out, and
begged her mistresses, as they sat at breakfast, to let her take the frizzes back and
change them. Her sister's daughter worked
in that very shop, and, though in the work-
room, would be able to oblige them, Hetty
was sure.

But the ladies looked at each other in
pleased assurance, and then turned together
to look at Hetty, who stood already a little
apprehensive near the table, where she had
just put down a plateful of smoking drop-
cakes. The good creature really began to
look old.

" They are worn very much in town," said

Miss Dobin. " We think it was quite fortunate that the fashion came in just as our hair was growing a trifle thin. I dare say we may choose those that are a shade duller in color when these are a little past. Oh, we shall · not want tea this evening, you remember, Hetty. I am glad there is likely to be such a good night for the sewing circle." And Miss Dobin and Miss Lucinda nodded and smiled.

" Oh, my sakes alive ! " the troubled handmaiden groaned. " Going to the circle, be they, to be snickered at ! Well, the Dobbin girls they was born, and the Dobbin girls they will remain till they die ; but if they ain't innocent Christian babes to those that knows 'em well, mark me down for an idjit myself ! They believe them front-pieces has set the clock back forty year or more, but if they 're pleased to think so, let 'em ! "

Away paced the Dulham ladies, late in the afternoon, to grace the parish occasion, and face the amused scrutiny of their neighbors. " I think we owe it to society to observe the fashions of the day," said Miss Lucinda. " A lady cannot afford to be unattractive. I feel now as if we were prepared for anything ! "

AN ONLY SON.

It was growing more and more uncomfortable in the room where Deacon Price had spent the greater part of a hot July morning. The sun did not shine in, for it was now directly overhead, but the glare of its reflection from the dusty village street and the white house opposite was blinding to the eyes. At least one of the three selectmen of Dalton, who were assembled in solemn conclave, looked up several times at the tops of the windows, and thought they had better see about getting some curtains.

There was more business than usual, but most of it belonged to the familiar detail of the office; there were bills to pay for the support of the town's-poor and the district schools, and, afterward, some discussion arose about a new piece of road which had been projected by a few citizens, who were as violently opposed by others. The selectmen were agreed upon this question, but they proposed to speak in private with the county commissioners, who were expected to view the region of the new highway the next week. This, however, had been well canvassed at their last meeting, and they had reached no new conclusions since ; so presently the conversation flagged a little, and Deacon Price drummed upon the ink-spattered table with his long, brown fingers, and John Kendall, the grist-miller, rose impatiently and went to the small window, where he stood with blinking eyes looking down into the street. His well-rounded figure made a pleasant shadow in that part of the room, but it seemed to grow hotter every moment. Captain Abel Stone left his chair impatiently, and taking his hat went down the short flight of stairs that led to the street, knocking his thick, shuffling boots clumsily by the way. He reached the sidewalk and looked up and down the street, but nobody was coming ; so he turned to Asa Ball, the shoemaker, who was standing in his shop-door.

"Business ain't brisk, I take it?" inquired the captain ; and Mr. Ball replied that he did n't do much more than tend shop, nowadays. Folks would keep on

buying cheap shoes, and thinking they
saved more money on two pair a year for
five dollars than when he used to make 'em
one pair for four. " But I make better pay
than I used to working at my trade, and so
I ain't going to fret," said Asa shrewdly,
with a significant glance at a modest pile of
empty cloth-boot boxes; and the captain
laughed a little, and took a nibble at a piece
of tobacco which he had found with much
difficulty in one of his deep coat pockets.
He had followed the sea in his early life,
but had returned to the small, stony farm
which had been the home of his childhood,
perhaps fifteen years before this story be-
gins. He had taken as kindly to inland
life as if he had never once been spattered
with sea water, and had been instantly
given the position in town affairs which
his wealth and character merited. He still
retained a good deal of his nautical way of
looking at things. One would say that to
judge by his appearance he had been well
rubbed with tar and salt, and it was supposed by his neighbors that his old sea-
chests were guardians of much money; he
was overrated by some of them as being
worth fifteen thousand dollars with the farm

thrown in. The captain was considered very peculiar, because he liked to live in the somewhat dilapidated little farmhouse, and some of his attempts at cultivating the sterile soil were the occasion of much amusement. He had made a large scrapbook, during his long sea-voyages, of all sorts of hints and suggestions for the tillage of the ground, gleaned from books and newspapers and almanacs, and nobody knows where else. He had pasted these in, or copied them in his stiff, careful handwriting, and pleased himself by watching his collection grow while he was looking forward through the long, storm-tossed years to his quiet anchorage among the Dalton hills. He was a single man, and though a braver never trod the quarter-deck, from motives of wisest policy he seldom opposed his will to that of Widow Martha Hawkes, who had consented to do him the great favor of keeping his house.

"Havin' a long session to-day, seems to me," observed the shoemaker, with little appearance of the curiosity which he really felt.

"There was a good many p'ints to be looked over," answered Captain Stone, becoming aware that he had secrets to guard, and looking impenetrable and unconcerned. "It's worked into a long drought, just as I said — I never took note of a drier sky; don't seem now as if we ever should get a sprinkle out of it, but I suppose we shall; " and he turned with a sigh to the door, and disappeared again up the narrow stairway. The three horses which were tied to adjacent posts in the full blaze of the sun all hung their ancient heads wearily, and solaced their disappointment as best they might. They had felt certain, when the captain appeared, that the selectmen's meeting was over. If they had been better acquainted with politics they might have wished that there could be a rising of the opposition, so that their masters would go out of office for as many years as they had come in.

The captain's companions looked up at him eagerly, as if they were sure that he was the herald of the expected tax-collector, who was to pay a large sum of money to them, of which the town treasury was in need. It was close upon twelve o'clock, and only a very great emergency would detain them beyond that time. They were growing very hungry, and when the captain, after a grave shake of his head, had settled into his chair again, they all felt more or less revengeful, though Deacon Price showed it by looking sad. One would have thought that he was waiting with reluctance to see some punishment descend upon the head of the delaying official.

"Well, Mis' Hawkes will be waiting dinner for me, and she never likes that," said Captain Stone at last; and just at that minute was heard the sound of wheels.

"Perhaps it's my mare stepping about, — she's dreadful restive in fly-time," suggested Mr. Kendall, and at once put his head out of the window; but when he took it in again, it was to tell his fellow-officers that Jackson was coming, and then they all sat solemnly in their chairs, with as much dignity as the situation of things allowed. Their judicial and governmental authority was plainly depicted in their expression. On ordinary occasions they were not remarkable, except as excellent old-fashioned countrymen; but when they represented to the world the personality and character of the town of Dalton, they would not have looked out of place seated in that stately company which Carpaccio has painted in the Reception of the English Embassadors. It was Dalton that gave audience that summer day, in the dusty, bare room, as Venice listens soberly in the picture.

They heard a man speak to his horse and leap to the ground heavily, and then listened eagerly to the clicks and fumblings which represented the tying of the halter, and then there were sounds of steps upon the stairway. The voice of Mr. Ball was heard, but it did not seem to have attracted much attention, and presently the long-waited-for messenger was in the room. He was dusty and sunburnt, and looked good-naturedly at his hosts. They greeted him amiably enough, and after he put his worn red handkerchief away he took a leather wallet from his pocket, and looking at a little roll of bills almost reluctantly turned them over with lingering fingers and passed them to Mr. Kendall, who sat nearest him, saying that he believed it was just right.

There was little else said, and after the money had again been counted the meeting was over. There was indeed a hurried arrangement as to who should guard the treasury, but when Deacon Price acknowledged that he meant to go to South Dalton next morning, he was at once deputed to carry the remittance to the bank there, where the town's funds and many of its papers already reposed. The deacon said slowly that he did n't know as he cared about keeping so much money in the house, but he was not relieved by either of his colleagues, and so these honest men separated and returned to private life again. Their homes were at some distance from each other; but for a half mile or so Deacon Price followed Captain Stone, and a cloud of dust followed them both. Then the captain turned to the left, up toward the hills; but Deacon Price kept on for some distance through the level lands, and at last went down a long lane, unshaded except here and there where some ambitious fence stakes had succeeded in changing themselves into slender willow-trees. In the spring the sides of the lane had been wet, and were full of green things, growing as fast as they could; but now these had been for some time dried up. The lane was bordered with dusty mayweed, and three deep furrows were worn through the turf, where the wagon wheels and the horse's patient feet had traveled back and forward so many years. The house stood at the end, looking toward the main road as if it wished it were there; it was a low-storied white house, with faded green blinds.

The deacon had tried to hurry his slow horse still more after he caught sight of another horse and wagon standing in the wide dooryard. He had entirely forgotten, until that moment, that his niece and housekeeper, Eliza Storrow, had made a final announcement in the morning that she was going to start early that afternoon for the next town to help celebrate a golden wedding. Poor Eliza had been somewhat irate because even this uncommon season of high festival failed to excite her uncle's love for society. She made him run the gauntlet, as usual on such occasions, by telling him successively that he took no interest in nobody and nothing, and that she was sure she should n't know what to say when people asked where he was; that it looked real unfeeling and cold-hearted, and he could n't expect folks to show any interest in him. These arguments, with many others, had been brought

forward on previous occasions until the deacon knew them all by heart, and he listened
to them impassively that morning, only ob-
serving cautiously to his son that Eliza
must go through with just so much. But
he promised to come back early from the
village, since Eliza and the cousin who was
to call for her meant to start soon after
twelve. It was a long drive, and they
wished to be in good season for the gathering of the clans.

He left the horse standing in the yard
and went into the house, feeling carefully at
his inner coat pocket as he did so. Eliza
had been watching for him, but the minute
he came in sight she had left the window
and begun to scurry about in the pantry.
The deacon did not stop to speak to her, but
went directly to his bedroom, and after a
moment's thought placed the precious wallet deep under the pillows. This act was
followed by another moment's reflection, and
as the old man turned, his son stood before
him in the doorway. Neither spoke; there
was a feeling of embarrassment which was
not uncommon between them; but presently
the young man said, " Eliza's been waiting
for you to have your dinner; she's in a great

hurry to get off. I 'll be in just as quick as I take care of the horse."

"You let her be ; I 'll put her up myself," said the deacon a little ungraciously. "I guess Eliza 'll get there soon enough. I should n't think she 'd want to start to ride way over there right in the middle of the day." At another time he would have been pleased with Warren's offer of aid, for that young man's bent was not in what we are pleased to call a practical direction. As he left the kitchen he noticed for the first time Mrs. Starbird, who sat by the farther window dressed in her best, and evidently brimming over with reproachful impatience. Deacon Price was a hospitable man, and stopped to shake hands with her kindly, and to explain that he had been delayed by some business that had come before the selectmen. He was politely assured that the delay was not of the least consequence, for Mrs. Starbird was going to drive the colt, and could make up the lost time on the road. As they stood talking, Eliza's footsteps were heard behind them, and, without turning or deigning to enter into any conversation with his niece, the deacon went out into the bright sunlight again.

Warren had preceded him after all, and was unfastening one of the traces, and his father unbuckled the other without a word. "You go in and have your dinner, — why won't you, father?" the young man said, looking up appealingly. "You need n't be afraid but I 'll do this all right."

"I declare, I was grieved when I saw, as I come up the lane, that you had n't mended up the fence there where I told you this forenoon. I had to be off, and there's the two calves right into the garden piece, and I don't know what works they 've been and done. It does seem too bad, Warren."

The son had worn a pleased and almost triumphant look, as if he had good news to tell, but now his face fell, and he turned crimson with shame and anger. "I would n't have forgot that for anything!" he stammered. "I 've been hurrying as fast as I could with something I 've been doing. I 'm going off" — but his father had already stepped inside the barn door with the hungry horse, and it was no use to say any more. Presently the deacon went into the house and ate his dinner, and after the few dishes had been washed, and Eliza had told him about the bread, and a piece of cold

boiled beef, and a row of blueberry pies, and
the sheet of gingerbread, which she had pro-
vided for the family's sustenance in her absence, she added that she might not be back
until early Wednesday morning, and then
she drove away in triumph with cousin Starbird.   It was the first holiday the good woman had had for more than a year, except
for church-going, and the deacon wished
her good-day with real affection and sympathy, having already asked if she had everything she wanted to carry over, and finally
desiring his respects to be given to the
folks.   He stood at the corner of the house
and watched her all the way down the lane
until she turned into the main road, and
Eliza herself was much pleased as she caught
sight of him.   She waved her hand gallantly, to which he responded by an almost
imperceptible inclination of the head and at
once turned away.

"There ain't a better man alive," said
cousin Starbird, whipping the elderly colt;
"he's as set as anybody I ever see, in his
own ways, but he's real good-hearted.   I
don't know anybody I'd look to quicker
than him if I got into misfortune.   He's
aged a good deal this last year, don't you

think he has, 'Liza? Sometimes I feel sure
that Warren's odd notions wears on him
more than we think."

"Course they do," said Eliza, throwing
back the shawl which she had felt obliged
to put on at first, out of respect to the occasion. "His father's mindful of Warren
every hour in the day. He is getting more
and more helpless and forgitful, and uncle's
growing feeble, and he ain't able either to
hire help or to do the farm work himself.
Sometimes Warren takes holt real good, but
it ain't often; and there he sets, up in that
room he's fixed over the wood-house, and
tinkers all day long. Last winter he used
to be there till late at night; he took out
one o' the window panes and set a funnel
out through, and used to keep a fire going
and a bright light up there till one or two
o'clock in the morning. His father never
slept a wink, I don't believe. He looks like
a man that's hard on to eighty, and he wa'n't
but sixty-seven his last birthday. I guess
Warren's teased him out of about all the
bank money he had put away. There! I
used to get interested myself in Warren's
notions about his machines, but now I can't
bear to hear him begin, and I go right into

the pantry and rattle round as if I was drove
to pieces."

"I suppose his father has indulged him
more, seeing that he was so much younger
than all the rest of his children, and they
being dead anyway. I declare, I never see
such a beautiful creatur' as Warren's mother
was. I always thought she was kind of
homesick here; 't was a lonesome place to
me, always, and I never counted on its being
healthy. The deacon 's begun to look kind
o' mossy, and I don't think. it 's all worry o'
mind. It 's kind of low land, and has always been called fevery." Cousin Starbird
was apt to look on the dark side of things.
" You can't always see the marks o' trouble,"
she went on. " There was old John Stacy,
that lost three children in one day with scarlet fever the fall after his wife died; then
his house got afire, and the bank failed where
his property was. Job himself could n't be
no worse off; and he took on dreadful, as
one thing after another came upon him, but
there wa'n't a younger appearing man of his
age anywhere at the time he died. He
seemed to spring right up again, like a bent
withe. I always thought it was a kind of a
pity that the deacon did n't push Warren

right off while he was young. He kept him
to home trying to make a farm-boy of him
till he was a grown man."

" Warren used to beseech him dreadfully
to let him go off, when I first come over to
live," said Eliza Storrow. " He had a great
notion of working in some kind of a machine shop, and they said that there wa'n't
so smart a workman there as he was; but
he got a notion that he could improve on
one of the machines, and lost all his interest
in workin' his trade, and the end of it was
that he spent a sight o' money to get a
patent, and found somebody had stepped in
with another just the week before. It was
an awful mean thing, too, for some thought
it was his notion that had been stole from
him. There was a fellow that boarded where
he did, to Lowell, that left all of a sudden,
and they thought he took the plan, — Warren being always free and pleasant with him,
— and then let somebody else have part of
it to get the patent through ; anyway it
was n't called for in any name they knew.
Warren was dreadful discouraged about it,
and was set against folks knowing, so don't
you never say nothing that I said about it.
I think he's kind of crazed about machin-

ery, and I don't believe he knows what he's
about more than half the time. He never
give me a misbeholden word, I'll say that
for him, but it's getting to be a melancholy
habitation if ever I see one," said Eliza
mournfully; and after this the conversation
turned to more hopeful themes relating to
the golden wedding.

The deacon had sighed as he turned away.
He wondered if they would make the twelve-
mile journey in safety, and smiled in spite
of himself as he remembered an old story.
He wished he had reminded them of those
two old women who were traveling from
Dalton to Somerset, and forgot where they
came from, and what their names were, and
where they were going. After this hidden
spring of humor had bubbled to the sur-
face, a little too late for anybody's enjoyment but his own, he relapsed into his usual
plaintive gravity, and, bringing a hammer
and nails and some stakes from the wood-
house, he went out to mend the broken fence.
It had been so often patched and propped
that it now seemed hardly to be repaired
again. The boards and posts had rotted
away, and the gamesome calves had forced
a wide breach in so weak a wall. It was a

half afternoon's work, and the day was hot,
but the tired old man set about it unflinch-
ingly, and took no rest until he had given
the topmost rail a shake and assured him.
self that it would last through his day. He
had brought more tools and pieces of board,
and he put these together to be replaced.
Just as he began his work he caught sight
of his son walking quickly away, far beyond
the house, across the pastures. The deacon
gave a heavy sigh, and as he hammered and
sawed and built his fence again, there had
been more than one sigh to follow it, for was
not this only son more strange and helpless
and useless than ever? There seemed little
to look forward to in life.

The garden was being sadly treated and
hindered by the drought; the beets and on-
ions were only half grown, and the reliable
old herb-bed seemed to have given up the
fight altogether. In one place there had
once been a flower-bed which belonged to
Warren's mother, but it was almost wholly
covered with grass. Eliza had no fondness
for flowers, and the two men usually were
unconscious that there were such things in
the world. But this afternoon the deacon

was glad to see a solitary sprig of London
Pride, which stood out in bold relief against
the gray post by the little garden gate. It
sent a bright ray of encouragement into the
shadow of his thoughts, and he went on his
way cheerfully. He told himself that next
he would attend to the wagon wheels, because he should need to start early in the
morning, in order to get home before the
heat of the day ; it was a hot piece of road
from here to the south village. He wondered idly where Warren had gone ; he was
glad he had not asked for money that day,
but he had done questioning his son about
his plans, or even the reason of his occa-
sional absences.

The side door, which led into the kitchen,
was shaded now, and a westerly breeze was
coming across the level fields, so the deacon
sat down on the doorstep to rest. The
old cat came out as if she wished for company, and rubbed against his arm and mewed
without making any noticeable sound. She
put her fore-feet on the old man's knee
and looked eagerly in his face and mewed
again inaudibly, and her master laughed and
wondered what she wanted. " I suppose the
cellar door is locked and bolted, and you

want to go down," said the deacon, "that's it, ain't it? I should ha' thought 'Liza would have rec'lected about them kittens, should n't you?" and pleasing himself with the creature's companionship, he rose and entered the house. The cat trotted alongside and disappeared quickly down the stairway, and, moved by some strange impulse, Deacon Price went into his bedroom to make sure that the wallet was safe under the pillow. He did not reach it at first, and he groped again, thinking that he had forgotten he pushed it so far under. But although he eagerly threw off the clothes and the pillows, and shook them twice over, and got down on his hands and knees and crept under the bed, and felt an odd singing noise grow louder and louder in his head, and at last became dizzy and dropped into the nearest chair, there was no wallet to be found.

Then he crept out into the empty kitchen, where the only sound was made by a fly that buzzed dismally in a spider's web. The air was close and hot in the house, and as the old man stood in the doorway it seemed as if there had some change come over his whole familiar world. He felt puzzled and weak, and at first started to go out

to the wagon with the vain hope of finding
the lost purse ; it might be that he — But
there was no use in imagining that he had
done anything but put it carefully under the
pillow, that his son had stood in the doorway as he lifted his head, and that the
money was gone. It was no use to deceive
himself, or to hunt through the house ; he
had always before his eyes the picture of the
pasture slope with the well-known figure of
his son following the path that led across it
to the nearest railroad station, a mile or two
away.

The daylight waned slowly, and the heat
of the sun lingered late into the night. Poor
John Price went through with his usual duties mechanically, but with perfect care, and
made the doing of his work last as long
as he could. The pig and the chickens and
the horse were fed ; then there were the
cows to bring in from pasture and to be
milked ; and at last the poor man even remembered the cat, and gave her a saucer of
milk for her supper ; but still it would not
grow dark, and still the shame and sorrow
weighed him down. In his restlessness he
went through the lower rooms of the house,
and opened the front door and shut it again,

and looked into the stiff little best room, and felt as if he were following the country custom, so familiar to him, of watching with the dead.

He did not get much sleep that night, in the uncomfortable bed which he tried to put into some sort of order before he lay down. Once he prayed aloud that the Lord would vouchsafe him a miracle, and that he might find his trust again, and what was still more precious, his confidence in his only son. For some reason he could not bear the sound of his own voice; and the thought of his time-honored office in the church pained him, for was it not disgraced and made a reproach?

Little by little the first sharpness of the shock wore away, while he tried to think what was to be done. The thought seized him that his son might have left some explanation of his going away, and he rose and took a candle and went to the little work-shop. There was less than the usual litter of cog-wheels and springs and screws, but somehow in the hot little room a feeling of reassurance and almost of hope took possession of him. It might be that Warren's hopes would not be disappointed, that he might be able to repay the stolen sum, that

he had only secreted it, and would return
later and give it back; for the poor deacon
assured himself over and over that he would
talk about the boy's affairs with him, and
try again to aid him and to put him into a
likely way at last, even if he had to mort-
gage the farm.

But in the morning, if there were still no
signs of the lad, what could be done? The
money which Jerry Jackson had owed the
town as tax-collector, and paid at last that
very day, — that seven hundred dollars; the
five hundred dollar bill, and the two that
stood for a hundred each, and some smaller
bills which were to pay the interest, — how
should they be replaced? He had no ready
money of any amount, nor would have until
the pay came for some hay, or unless he
could persuade a neighbor, whose payments
were honest but slow, to take up a note given
for a piece of outlying woodland sold the
winter before.

All through that long summer night he
worried and waited for the morning, and
sometimes told himself that his only son had
robbed him, and sometimes said that Warren would never serve him like that, and
when he came home it would be all made

right. The whippoorwills were singing about the house, and one even came to perch on the kitchen doorstep and repeat its accusing cry. The waning moon rose late, and made a solemn red light in the east, and shone straight in at the little bedroom window as if it were a distant bale-fire on the hills. A little dog kept up a fierce barking by the next farmhouse, far away across the fields, and at last the tired man was ready to think his miserable wakefulness was the fault of the cur. . . . Yes, he had given Warren all the money he could, he had meant well by the boy, and surely now, unless the poor fellow had gone mad, there would be some way out of all this trouble ; at any rate, he would not let other people have a chance to call his son a thief until there was no help for it.

The next morning, after a short, uneasy sleep, from which the deacon had a sad awaking, he hungrily ate some breakfast at the pantry shelves, and harnessed the old horse, and set out on a day's journey of which he hardly knew the end. He shut the door of the house and locked it, and gave a look of lingering affection at the old place, even stopping the horse for a minute in the lane that he might turn to survey it

again most carefully.   He felt as if he were
going to do it wrong, and as if it were a conscious thing, the old weather-beaten dwelling
that had sheltered him all his life, and those
who had been dearest to him.   It had no
great attractions for a stranger.   It was a
representative house for that somewhat primitive farming region, though it had fallen
out of repair, and wore a damaged and re-
sourceless aspect.   The appearance of a
man's home is exactly characteristic of himself.   Human nature is more powerful than
its surroundings, and shapes them inevitably
to itself.

It was still very early in the morning, and
few persons were stirring.   In fact, Deacon
Price met nobody on the road except a
sleepy boy following his cows to pasture,
and he did not feel like looking him in the
face, but gave a pull at the reins to hurry
the horse and pass by without question.
He took a cross road that was cool and
shady at that hour, and while he journeyed
slowly up the rough by-way he let the horse
choose its own course without guidance.
Some birds were crying and calling in the
woods close by, as if it were altogether a
day of ill omen and disaster.   John Price

felt more and more as if his world was coming to an end, and everything was going to
pieces. He never had understood his son
very well; there are some people who are
like the moon, with one side always hidden
and turned away, and Warren was only half
familiar to his father. The old man had
been at first inclined to treat his bright boy
with a sort of respect and reverence, but in
later years this had changed little by little
to impatience and suspicion. It had been a
great mortification that he had been obliged
to maintain him, and once when somebody,
perhaps Eliza Storrow, had been comment-
ing upon a certain crop of wild oats which
a neighboring lad had arranged for his har-
vesting, the deacon was heard to mutter,
" Better them than no crop at all! " Yet he
had never suffered his acquaintances to com-
ment upon his son's behavior; his own treatment of him in public had insisted upon the
rendering of respect from other people, but
he had not acknowledged to himself, until
this last sad night, that there was no practical result to be hoped for from Warren's
gifts and graces. This might have been
borne, and they might have struggled on together, somehow or other, but for this terri-

ble blow of the theft of the town's money,
which now left a debt and sorrow on the old
man's shoulders almost too heavy to be
borne.

In a short time the woods were passed,
and the road led out to a pleasant country of
quite different character from the lowland
neighborhood left behind. There were gently
sloping hills and long lines of elms, and the
farms looked more prosperous. One farm
only on this road was unproductive, and this
was partly the fault of art, and partly of
nature, for it was the homestead of Captain
Stone, a better sailor than farmer. Its pastures were gathering-places for the ledges,
and the fields were all made swampy by
many springs. It seemed to be the waste
corner of that region for all unused and
undeveloped materials of farming land; but
while there was every requisite, there was a
chaotic and primitive arrangement of clay,
rock, and sand. Yet the captain had settled
down here in blissful content as a tiller of the
soil; and while he might have bought the
best farm in the county, he congratulated
himself upon his rare privileges here, and
would have found more level and kindly
acres as uninteresting as being becalmed in

tropic seas. He worked his farm as he had
sailed his ships, by using tact and discretion,
and with true seaman's philosophy he never
fretted. He waited for the wind to change,
or the tide of spring to flow, or of winter to
ebb, for he had long ago learned there was
no hurrying nature; and to hear him talk
of one of his small plots of thin hay, or
slow - growing potatoes, you would have
thought it an intelligent creature which existed mainly on his benevolent encouragement and tolerance. By some persons the
captain was laughed at, and by others he
was condemned. The trouble was that he
had a shrewd insight into human nature,
and was so impossible to deceive or to persuade against his will that he had made
many enemies, who had hoped to grow rich
by emptying the good old man's pockets.

It was to this lifelong friend that Deacon
Price had turned in his extremity; but as
he drew nearer that morning to the red
house on the hilltop, his heart began to fail
him, for what if he should be refused!
There seemed no other resource, in such a
case, but to make the sad occurrence known,
or to go away in search of Warren himself.
He could put the deeds of his farm, those

worn deeds that had come down from father
to son, generation after generation, into the
hands of the other selectmen, who would be
sure to stand his friends and keep the secret
for a time. Warren had looked discouraged,
and pale, and desperate in the last month,
and his father suddenly remembered this, and
groaned aloud as he wished that the boy had
come to him, and that he had made it possible, instead of coldly ignoring and disap-
proving him day after day; such a mixture
of wrath and shame and compassion has
seldom been in a father's heart.

The captain was abroad early, and the
deacon saw him first, sauntering about at
the foot of the slope on which his house and
buildings stood. He seemed to be examining
the soil, and greeted his guest with a hearty
satisfaction. The deacon slowly alighted,
and leaving his trusty steed to gnaw the
fence or browse among the bushes as she
chose, went into the field. He walked
feebly, and when he met the captain he
could hardly find words to tell his errand.
Men of his kind are apt to be made silent
by any great occurrence; they have rarely
anything but a limited power of expression,

and their language only serves them for common use. Those who have lived close to nature understand each other without speech, as dogs or horses do, and the elder generations of New Englanders knew less of society and human companionship and association than we can comprehend.

The captain watched his visitor as he came toward him, and when they met he gave one quick, final look, and then proceeded to make use of his usual forms of greeting, as if he had no idea that anything was the matter.

"I've taken a notion to set out some cramb'ries hereabouts another year," he announced. "I never made a voyage to sea without cramb'ries aboard, if I could help myself. They last well, and taste sprightly when other things is begun to lose savor. I don't cut any hay to speak of, in this piece. I 've been meaning to tackle it somehow — See here," — pushing it with his great foot, — "it 's all coming up brakes and sedge. I do' know 's you want to be standing about — It *is* master spongy for good grass land, and 't would be a great expense to drain it off. I s'pose I 'm gettin' too old to try any of these new notions, but they sort of divert me. We're having a bad spell o' drought, ain't we? 'T is all tops of rocks about here, and we're singed pretty brown." The captain chattered more briskly than was his wont; it was impossible to mistake the fact of his being a sailor, for indeed that business stamps its followers with an unmistakable brand.

They ventured upon a wetter spot than usual, and when the deacon pulled up his foot from the mire underneath with a resounding plop, his host proposed that they should seek the higher ground.

"Pretty smart at home?" asked the captain presently, to end a season of strange silence; and the deacon replied, at first somewhat sorrowfully, that they were fair to middling, but explained directly that Eliza was away for a couple of nights, and Warren too; it cost a great effort to speak the young man's name.

"Oh, yes, I rec'lect," growled the captain amiably. "You spoke about the golden weddin' yisterday; I should thought you'd ha' gone too, along with 'Liza; such junkets ain't to be had every day. I must say I wish something or other would happen to take Mis' Hawkes's attention off of me," dropping his voice cautiously, as they came nearer to the house. "She's had a dreadful grumpy time of it, this week past, and looked homely enough to stop a clock. I used to be concerned along in the first of it, when I come off the sea, but I found it did n't do no hurt, and so I let her work, and first thing you know the wind is veered round again handsome, and off you go."

The deacon tried to laugh at this; the friends seated themselves on the off side of the wood-pile, under the shade of a great choke-pear tree. They had mounted the chopping-block, which was a stout elm log, standing on six legs, so that it looked like some stupid, blunderheaded creature of not altogether harmless disposition. The two old men were quite at its mercy if it should canter away suddenly; but they talked for some minutes on ordinary subjects, and even left their position to go to inspect the pigs, and returned again, before the deacon arrived at an explanation of his errand.

It was a hard thing to do, and the captain turned and looked at him narrowly.

"I 've got to use the money right away as soon as I can have it. I want to see to some business this forenoon; you know I 've

been calc'latin' to go to the south village
to-day anyway. I did n't know for certain I
should have to see about this, or I would n't
have given you such short notice " — and
here the deacon stopped again; it had come
very near an untruth, this last sentence,
and he would not cheat the man of whom
he was asking so great a favor.

" I did n't fetch the papers along because
I did n't know how 't would be with you,"
he explained; "they'll make you safe.
Austin's folks was talking round, this
spring, to see if I wanted to part with our
north field; his youngest son's a smart
fellow, and wants to set up for himself and
have a truck farm. But I 'm only asking
the loan for a time, ye know, neighbor,"
and the deacon looked anxiously at the old
captain, and then leaned over, poking the
chips about with the butt of his whip, which
he had brought with him from the wagon.

" You shall have it," said the captain at
last. " 'T ain't everybody I 'd do such a
thing to obleege, and I am only going to
have my say about one thing, John : I never
had no family of my own, and I suppose the
feelin's of a father are somethin' I don't
know nothing about, for or against; but I

must say I hate to see ye an old man before your time, runnin' all out and looking
discouraged on account o' favorin' Warren.
You'll come in astern o' the lighter, and he
too; and if he's been beseechin' ye to get
this money together to further his notions,
I'm doing ye both a wrong to let ye have
it. But I can't deny ye, and I've got more
than what ye say ye want, right here in the
house as it happens. I was going to buy
into that new three-masted schooner the
Otises have got on the stocks now; I don't
know but I am getting along in years to
take hold of anything new in navigation."

"I ain't intending to let Warren have
none o' this," said the deacon humbly, and
he longed to say more, and felt as if he
never could hold up his head again among
his fellows; and the time seemed very long
and dreary before the captain came back
from his house with the note ready to sign,
and the seven hundred dollars ready to place
in the deacon's gray and shaking hand.
His benefactor pondered long over this
strange visit, longing to know what had
happened, but he assured himself over and
over that he couldn't help letting him have
it, and if never a cent of it came back there

was nobody he was gladder to oblige. And John Price took his weary way to the south village of Dalton, and paid a sum of seven hundred and thirty-five dollars to the creditors of the town. It was not until early in the afternoon that old Abel Stone suddenly bethought himself that something might have happened about that payment of Jerry Jackson's. If he were not growing old and a fool at last! Why had n't he asked the deacon if he had lost the money he had taken home from the selectmen's office! And when Mrs. Hawkes afterward ventured to ask him a harmless question, he had grown red in the face and poured forth a torrent of nautical language which had nearly taken her breath away, without apparent reason or excuse. The captain, it must be confessed, was an uncommon swearer; he was one of the people who seem to serve as volcanoes, or outlets for the concealed anger of poor human nature. It is difficult to explain why profanity seems so much more unlawful and shocking in some persons than in others, but there was something fairly amusing in the flurry and sputter of irreverent words which betokened excitement of any kind in the mind of Cap-

tain Stone. He even forgot himself so far
as to swear a little occasionally in the course
of earnest exhortations in the evening
prayer-meetings. There was not a better
man or a sincerer Christian in the town of
Dalton, though he had become a church-
member late in life; and knowing this,
there was never anything but a compassionate smile when he grew red in the face with
zeal, and recommended the poor damned
dogs of heathen to mercy.

Nothing seemed to have changed out-
wardly at the south village. John Price
did his errands and finished his business as
quickly as possible, and avoided meeting his
acquaintances, for he could not help fearing
that he should be questioned about this miserable trouble. As he left the bank he
could not help giving a sigh of relief, for
that emergency was bridged over; and for
a few minutes he kept himself by main force
from looking at the future, or asking himself
" What next ? "

But as he turned into his dust-powdered
lane again at noon, the curious little faces of
the mayweed blossoms seemed to stare up at
him, and there was nobody to speak to him,

and the house was like a tomb where all the years of his past were lying dead, and all the pleasantness of life existed only in remembrance.

He began to wish for Warren in an unexpected way; and as he looked about the house he saw everywhere some evidence of his son's mechanical skill. Had not Eliza Storrow left home without a fear because, as she always said, Warren was as handy as a woman? The remembrance of such patient diligence at his own chosen work, his quietness under reproof, his evident discomfort at having to be dependent upon his father, linked to a perfect faith in the ultimate success of his plans, — the thought of all these things flashed through the old man's mind. "I wish I had waited 'til he told me what he had to say, yisterday," said Deacon Price to himself. " 'T was strange about that fence too. He 's al'ays been willing to take holt and help whenever I spoke to him." He even came to believe that the boy had grown desperate, and in some emergency had gone in search of new materials for his machine. "He 's so forgitful," said the father, " he may have forgot to speak about the money, and 't was but a small-looking roll of bills.

He 'll be back to-night, like 's not, as concerned as can be when he finds out what 't was
he took." It was the way we remember only
the good qualities of our friends who have
died, and let the bad ones fade out of sight,
and so know the angels that were growing in
them all the while, and have thrown off the
disguise and hindrance of the human shape.

Towards evening Jacob Austin, a neighbor, came into the yard on an errand, and
was astonished to see how tired and old the
deacon looked. He had left the oxen and
their great load of coarse meadow hay standing in the road at the end of the lane, and
meant at first to shoulder the borrowed pitchfork and quickly rejoin them, but it was impossible. He asked if anything were the
matter, and was answered that there was
something trying about such a long spell of
drought, which did not in the least satisfy
his curiosity.

"No," said the deacon, " I 'm getting to
be an old man, but I keep my health fairly.
Eliza and Warren, they 're both off 'tending
to their own concerns, but I make sure one
or both of 'm 'll be back toward sundown."
And Jacob, after casting about in his mind

for anything further to say, mentioned again that 't was inconvenient to break a pitchfork right in the middle of loading a rack, and went away.

"Looked to me as if he had had a stroke," he told his family that night at supper-time; and the conduct of Warren and Eliza Storrow, in going off and leaving the old deacon to shift for himself, was most severely commented upon.

But all this time, the latter half of that Tuesday afternoon, Eliza and her cousin Starbird were jogging toward home over the Dalton and Somerset hills. The colt was in good trim, and glad to be nearing his own familiar stall again, and struck out at an uncommonly good pace, though none of the swiftest at that. It was hardly six o'clock when the two tired-out and severely sunburnt women came into the yard. The deacon heard the high-pitched voice which he knew so well, before he heard the sound of the wheels on the soft, dry turf, and went out to greet the new-comers, half glad and half afraid. Eliza took it for granted that Warren was either in the workshop as usual, or, as she scornfully expressed it, roaming the hills, and did not ask for him. Cousin

Starbird had accepted an invitation to tea,
as her home was three miles farther on.
They were both heavy women, and stiff
from sitting still so long in the old wagon,
and they grumbled a little as they walked
toward the house.

"Yes, 't was a splendid occasion," Eliza
answered the deacon, as he stood near, hitch-
ing the colt to a much gnawed post. "It all
went off beautifully. Everybody wanted to
know where you was, an' Warren. There,
we talked till we was all about dead, and eat
ourselves sick; you never saw a handsomer
table in *your* life. The old folks stood it
well, but I see they 'd begun to kind o' give
out at dinner-time to-day, — last night was
the celebration, you know, because some
could come in the evenin' that was occupied
by day. They wanted us to stop longer, but
I see 't was best to break it up, and I 'd rather
go over again by an' by, and spend the day
in peace an' quietness, and have a good visit.
We 've been saying, as we rode along, that
we should n't be surprised if the old folks
kind o' faded out after this, they 've been
lookin' forward to it so long. Well, it 's
all over, like a hoss-race; " and Eliza heaved
a great sigh and went into the front room to

open the blinds and make it less stuffy; then she removed her best bonnet in her own room, and presently came out to get tea, dressed in her familiar everyday calico gown.

The deacon was sitting by the open window, drumming on the sill; he had a trick of beating a slow tattoo with the ends of his queerly shaped fingers. They were long and dry, and somehow did not look as if they were useful, though John Price had been a hard-working man. Cousin Starbird had come downstairs first, and had gone out to find a piece of the golden wedding cake that had been left in the wagon. Eliza was busy in the pantry, scolding a good deal at the state she found it in.

"Whatever is this great thing in my pocket!" she exclaimed, for something had struck the table-leg as she came by it to bring the last brace of blueberry pies; then quickly fumbling in the pocket's depths she took out the deacon's great brown wallet, and presented it to its owner.

"Good King Agrippy!" said the amazed man, snatching it, and looking at Eliza angrily and then at the wallet again, and turning it over in his hand.

" I ain't give it a thought, from that minute to this," said Eliza, who was not a little frightened. " I s'pose you 've been thinking you lost it. I thought you looked dreadful wamblecropped when I first saw you. Why, you see, I did n't undertake to wash yesterday mornin', because I did n't want the clothes a-layin' and mildewin', and I kind of thought perhaps I 'd put it off till next week, anyway, though it ain't my principle to do fortnight's washes. An' I had so much to do, gettin' ready to start, that I 'd gone in early and made up your bed and not put a clean sheet on ; but you was busy takin' out the hoss after you come home at noon, and had your dinner to eat, and I had the time to spare, so I just slipped in and stripped off the bedclothes then, and this come out from under the pillow. I meant to hand it to you when you come in from the barn, but I forgot it the next minute ; you know we was belated about starting, and I was scatter-witted. I hope it ain't caused you no great inconvenience ; you ain't wanted it for anything very special, have you ? I s'pose 't was foolish to go fussin' about the bed, but I thought if you should be sick or anything " —

" Well, I 've got it now," said the deacon,
drawing a long breath. " I own I felt some
uneasy about it." Presently he went out to
the yard, and across the garden, and beyond
the garden to the family burying-lot in the
field. He would have gone to his parish
church to pray if he had been a devout
Catholic; as it was, this was the nearest approach he could make to a solemn thanksgiving.

Some of the oldest stones lay flat on the
ground, and a network of blackberry vines
covered them in part. The leaves were
burnt by the sun, and the crickets scrambled
among them as the deacon's foot-fall startled
them. His first wife and his second wife
both were buried there, their resting-places
marked by a slate head-stone and a marble
one, and it was to this last that the old man
went. His first wife had been a plain, hard-
worked woman of sterling worth, and his
fortunes had declined from the day she left
him to guard them alone ; but her successor
had been a pale and delicate school-teacher,
who had roused some unsuspected longing
for beauty and romance in Deacon Price's
otherwise prosaic nature. She had seemed
like a windflower growing beside a ledge ;

and her husband had been forced to confess
that she was not fit for a farmer's wife. If
he could have had a combination of his two
partners, he had once ventured to think, he
would have been exactly suited. But it
seemed to him, as he stood before the grave
with his head bowed, the only way of making some sign of his sorrow, he had wrong-
fully accused an innocent man, his son and
hers; and there he stayed, doing penance as
best he could, until Eliza's voice called him
to the house, and to some sort of comfortable existence and lack of self-reproof.

Before they had finished supper Warren
came in, looking flushed and tired; but he
took his seat at the table after a pleasant
greeting, and the deacon passed him every
plate within reach, treating him with uncommon politeness. The father could not
help noticing that his son kept stealing
glances at him, and that he looked pleased
and satisfied. It seemed to him as if Warren must have known of his suspicions and
of their happy ending, but it was discovered
presently that the long-toiled-over machine
had proved to be a success. Warren had
taken it to his former employer at Lowell,
who gladly promised, so great was his de-

light with it, to pay the expenses of getting
a patent in exchange for a portion of the
right. "He said there would be no end to
the sale of it," said the young man, looking
eagerly at his father's face. "I would n't
have run off so yesterday, but I was so full
of it I could n't bear to think of losing the
cars, and I did n't want to say one word
about this thing till I was sure.

"I expect I have been slack," he continued with evident effort, while they leaned
over the garden fence, and he looked at his
father appealingly. "But the fact is, I
could n't seem to think of other things ; it
took all there was of me to keep right after
that. But now I 'm going to take right
hold and be some help about the place. I
don't seem to want to touch a tool again
for a year." Warren looked pale and rest-
less ; the reaction from his long excitement
had set in.

The deacon gave a shaky laugh, and struck
his son's shoulder by way of a clumsy caress.
"Don't you go to frettin' yourself now," he
said. "I ain't felt so pleased as I do to-
day since the day you come into the world.
I sort of felt certain then that you was goin'
to be somebody, I do' know why 't was,"

—and he turned away suddenly toward the house. "If you are as rich as you say you be, I should n't wonder if between us we had n't better get them blinds painted, and smart us up a little, another year. I declare, the old place has begun to look considerable gone to seed."

That night a great thunder-shower broke the spell of the long drought, and afterward, until morning, the rain fell fast upon the thirsty ground. It was a good night to sleep, Eliza said, as she wearily climbed the crooked backstairs at nine o'clock, for there was already a coolness in the air. Eliza never was told the whole of the story about the wallet, for when she heard part of it she only said it was just like a man, — they were generally the most helpless creatur's alive. The deacon might have known she had put it away somewhere. Why did n't he come and ask her? He never seemed to mistrust that it was a direct p'inting out of his duty to ride over to Somerset to the gathering, and just speak to the folks.

In the early morning, while it was cool and wet, Deacon Price drove up to Captain Stone's farm, and the two selectmen perched on the chopping-log again, while the confession was made and listened to with great gravity. The captain swore roundly in his satisfaction, and said he was going to have a square talk with Warren, and advise with him a little, for fear that those landsharks down in Lowell should undertake to cheat him. He stowed away the repayment of the loan in one of his big pockets, as if it were of little consequence to him, but he announced with considerable satisfaction at the next selectmen's meeting, that he owned a few planks of that three-masted schooner which the Otises were about ready to launch. And he winked at Deacon Price in a way that their brother Kendall was not able to understand.

MARSH ROSEMARY.

I.

ONE hot afternoon in August, a single moving figure might have been seen following a straight road that crossed the salt marshes of Walpole. Everybody else had either stayed at home or crept into such shade as could be found near at hand. The thermometer marked at least ninety degrees. There was hardly a fishing-boat to be seen on the glistening sea, only far away on the hazy horizon two or three coasting schooners looked like ghostly Flying Dutchmen, becalmed for once and motionless.

Ashore, the flaring light of the sun brought out the fine, clear colors of the level landscape. The marsh grasses were a more vivid green than usual, the brown tops of those that were beginning to go to seed looked almost red, and the soil at the edges of the tide inlets seemed to be melting into a black, pitchy substance like the dark pigments on a painter's palette. Where the land was higher the hot air flickered above it dizzily. This was not an afternoon that one would naturally choose for a long walk, yet Mr. Jerry Lane stepped briskly forward, and appeared to have more than usual energy. His big boots trod down the soft carpet of pussy-clover that bordered the dusty, whitish road. He struck at the stationary procession of thistles with a little stick as he went by. Flight after flight of yellow butterflies fluttered up as he passed, and then wavered down again to their thistle flowers, while on the shiny cambric back of Jerry's Sunday waistcoat basked at least eight large green-headed flies in complete security.

It was difficult to decide why the Sunday waistcoat should have been put on that Saturday afternoon. Jerry had not thought it important to wear his best boots or best trousers, and had left his coat at home altogether. He smiled as he walked along, and once when he took off his hat, as a light breeze came that way, he waved it triumphantly before he put it on again. Evidently this was no common errand that led him due west, and made him forget the hot weather, and caused him to shade his eyes with his hand, as he looked eagerly at a clump of trees and the chimney of a small house a littleway beyond the boundary of the marshes, where the higher ground began.

Miss Ann Floyd sat by her favorite window, sewing, twitching her thread less decidedly than usual, and casting a wistful glance now and then down the road, or at the bees in her gay little garden outside. There was a grim expression overshadowing her firmly-set, angular face, and the frown that always appeared on her forehead when she sewed or read the newspaper was deeper and straighter than usual. She did not look as if she were conscious of the heat, though she had dressed herself in an old-fashioned skirt of sprigged lawn and a loose jacket of thin white dimity with out-of-date flowing sleeves. Her sandy hair was smoothly brushed; one lock betrayed a slight crinkle at its edge, but it owed nothing to any encouragement of Nancy Floyd's. A hard, honest, kindly face this was, of a woman whom everybody trusted, who might be expected to give of whatever she had to give, good measure, pressed down and running over. She was a lonely soul; she had no near relatives in the world. It seemed always as if nature had been mistaken in not planting her somewhere in a large and busy household.

The little square room, kitchen in winter and sitting-room in summer, was as clean and bare and thrifty as one would expect the dwelling-place of such a woman to be. She sat in a straight-backed, splint-bottomed kitchen chair, and always put back her spool with a click on the very same spot on the window-sill. You would think she had done with youth and with love affairs, yet you might as well expect the ancient cherry-tree in the corner of her yard to cease adventuring its white blossoms when the May sun shone! No woman in Walpole had more bravely and patiently borne the burden of loneliness and lack of love. Even now her outward behavior gave no hint of the new excitement and delight that filled her heart.

"Land sakes alive!" she says to herself presently, "there comes Jerry Lane. I expect, if he sees me settin' to the winder, he 'll come in an' dawdle round till supper-time!" But good Nancy Floyd smooths her hair hastily as she rises and drops her work, and steps back toward the middle of the room, watching the gate anxiously all the time. Now, Jerry, with a crestfallen look at the vacant window, makes believe that he is going by, and takes a loitering step or two onward, and then stops short; with a somewhat sheepish smile he leans over the neat picket fence and examines the blue and white and pink larkspur that covers most of the space in the little garden. He takes off his hat again to cool his forehead, and replaces it, without a grand gesture this time, and looks again at the window hopefully. There is a pause. The woman knows that the man is sure she is there; a little blush colors her thin cheeks as she comes boldly to the wide-open front door.

"What do you think of this kind of weather?" asks Jerry Lane complacently, as he leans over the fence, and surrounds himself with an air of self-sacrifice.

"I call it hot," responds the Juliet from her balcony, with deliberate assurance, " but the corn needs sun, everybody says. I should n't have wanted to toil up from the shore under such a glare, if I had been you.

Better come in and set awhile, and cool off,"
she added, without any apparent enthusiasm.
Jerry was sure to come, anyway. She would
rather make the suggestion than have him.

Mr. Lane sauntered in, and seated himself opposite his hostess, beside the other
small window, and watched her admiringly
as she took up her sewing and worked at it
with great spirit and purpose. He clasped
his hands together and leaned forward a
little. The shaded kitchen was very comfortable, after the glaring light outside, and
the clean orderliness of the few chairs, and
the braided rugs, and the table under the
clock, with some larkspur and asparagus in
a china vase for decoration, seemed to please
him unexpectedly. "Now just see what
ways you women folks have of fixing things
up smart!" he ventured gallantly.

Nancy's countenance did not forbid further compliment; she looked at the flowers
herself, quickly, and explained that she had
gathered them a while ago to send to the
minister's sister, who kept house for him.
"I saw him going by, and expected he 'd be
back this same road. Mis' Elton 's be'n
havin' another o' her dyin' spells this noon,
and the deacon went by after him hot foot.

I 'd souse her well with stone-cold water.
She never sent for me to set up with her ;
she knows better. Poor man, 't was likely
he was right into the middle of to-morrow's
sermon. 'T ain't considerate of the deacon,
and when he knows he 's got a fool for a
wife, he need n't go round persuading other
folks she 's so suffering as she makes out.
They ain't got no larkspur this year to the
parsonage, and I was going to let the minister take this over to Amandy ; but I see his
wagon over on the other road, going towards
the village, about an hour after he went by
here."

It seemed to be a relief to tell somebody
all these things after such a season of forced
repression, and Jerry listened with gratify-
ing interest. " How you do see through
folks ! " he exclaimed in a mild voice. Jerry
could be very soft spoken if he thought best.
" Mis' Elton 's a die-away lookin' creatur'.
I heard of her saying last Sunday, comin'
out o' meetin', that she made an effort to git
there once more, but she expected 't would
be the last time. Looks as if she eat well,
don't she ? " he concluded in a meditative
tone.

" Eat ! " exclaimed the hostess, with snap-

ping eyes. " There ain't no woman in town,
sick or well, can lay aside the food that she
does. 'T ain't to the table afore folks, but
she goes seeking round in the cupboards
half a dozen times a day. An' I 've heard
her remark 't was the last time she ever
expected to visit the sanctuary as much as
a dozen times within five years."

" Some places I 've sailed to they 'd have
hit her over the head with a club long ago,"
said Jerry, with an utter lack of sympathy
that was startling. " Well, I must be gettin' back again. Talkin' of eatin' makes us
think o' supper-time. Must be past five,
ain't it? I thought I 'd just step up to see
if there wa'n't anything I could lend a hand
about, this hot day."

Sensible Ann Floyd folded her hands over
her sewing, as it lay in her lap, and looked
straight before her without seeing the pleading face of the guest. This moment was a
great crisis in her life. She was conscious
of it, and knew well enough that upon her
next words would depend the course of future events. The man who waited to hear
what she had to say was indeed many years
younger than she, was shiftless and vacillat-
ing. He had drifted to Walpole from no-

body knew where, and possessed many qualities which she had openly rebuked and despised in other men. True enough, he was
good-looking, but that did not atone for the
lacks of his character and reputation. Yet
she knew herself to be the better man of the
two, and since she had surmounted many ob-
stacles already she was confident that, with
a push here and a pull there to steady him,
she could keep him in good trim. The win-
ters were so long and lonely; her life was
in many ways hungry and desolate in spite
of its thrift and conformity. She had
laughed scornfully when he stopped, one day
in the spring, and offered to help her weed
her garden; she had even joked with one
of the neighbors about it. Jerry had been
growing more and more friendly and pleasant ever since. His ease-loving, careless nature was like a comfortable cushion for hers,
with its angles, its melancholy anticipations
and self-questionings. But Jerry liked her,
and if she liked him and married him, and
took him home, it was nobody's business;
and in that moment of surrender to Jerry's
cause she arrayed herself at his right hand
against the rest of the world, ready for war-
fare with any and all of its opinions.

She was suddenly aware of the sunburnt face and light, curling hair of her undeclared lover, at the other end of the painted table with its folded leaf. She smiled at him vacantly across the larkspur; then she gave a little start, and was afraid that her thoughts had wandered longer than was seemly. The kitchen clock was ticking faster than usual, as if it were trying to attract attention.

"I guess I'll be getting home," repeated the visitor ruefully, and rose from his chair, but hesitated again at an unfamiliar expression upon his companion's face.

"I don't know as I've got anything extra for supper, but you stop," she said, "an' take what there is. I wouldn't go back across them marshes right in this heat."

Jerry Lane had a lively sense of humor, and a queer feeling of merriment stole over him now, as he watched the mistress of the house. She had risen, too; she looked so simple and so frankly sentimental, there was such an incongruous coyness added to her usually straightforward, angular appearance, that his instinctive laughter nearly got the better of him, and might have lost him the prize for which he had been waiting these many months. But Jerry behaved like a man : he stepped forward and kissed Ann Floyd ; he held her fast with one arm as he stood beside her, and kissed her again and again. She was a dear good woman. She had a fresh young heart, in spite of the straight wrinkle in her forehead and her work-worn hands. She had waited all her days for this joy of having a lover.

II.

EVEN Mrs. Elton revived for a day or two under the tonic of such a piece of news. That was what Jerry Lane had hung round for all summer, everybody knew at last. Now he would strike work and live at his ease, the men grumbled to each other ; but all the women of Walpole deplored most the weakness and foolishness of the elderly bride. Ann Floyd was comfortably off, and had something laid by for a rainy day ; she would have done vastly better to deny herself such an expensive and utterly worthless luxury as the kind of husband Jerry Lane would make. He had idled away his life. He earned a little money now and then in

seafaring pursuits, but was too lazy, in the
shore parlance, to tend lobster-pots. What
was energetic Ann Floyd going to do with
him? She was always at work, always equal
to emergencies, and entirely opposed to
dullness and idleness and even placidity.
She often avowed scornfully that she liked
people who had some snap to them, and now
she had chosen for a husband the laziest
man in Walpole. "Dear sakes," one woman said to another, as they heard the news,
"there's no fool like an old fool!"

The days went quickly by, while Miss
Ann made her plain wedding clothes. If
people expected her to put on airs of youth
they were disappointed. Her wedding bonnet was the same sort of bonnet she had
worn for a dozen years, and one disappointed critic deplored the fact that she had
spruced up so little, and kept on dressing
old enough to look like Jerry Lane's mother.
As her acquaintances met her they looked
at her with close scrutiny, expecting to see
some outward trace of such a silly, uncharacteristic departure from good sense and
discretion. But Miss Floyd, while she was
still Miss Floyd, displayed no silliness and
behaved with dignity, while on the Sunday

after a quiet marriage at the parsonage she and Jerry Lane walked up the side aisle together to their pew, the picture of middle-aged sobriety and respectability. Their fellow-parishioners, having recovered from their first astonishment and amusement, settled down to the belief that the newly married pair understood their own business best, and that if anybody could make the best of Jerry and get any work out of him, it was his capable wife.

"And if she undertakes to drive him too hard he can slip off to sea, and they 'll be rid of each other," commented one of Jerry's 'longshore companions, as if it were only reasonable that some refuge should be afforded to those who make mistakes in matrimony.

There did not seem to be any mistake at first, or for a good many months afterward. The husband liked the comfort that came from such good housekeeping, and enjoyed a deep sense of having made a good anchorage in a well-sheltered harbor, after many years of thriftless improvidence and drifting to and fro. There were some hindrances to perfect happiness: he had to forego long seasons of gossip with his particular friends, and the outdoor work which was expected of him, though by no means heavy for a person of his strength, fettered his freedom not a little. To chop wood, and take care of a cow, and bring a pail of water now and then, did not weary him so much as it made him practically understand the truth of weakly Sister Elton's remark, that life was a constant chore. And when poor Jerry, for lack of other interest, fancied that his health was giving way mysteriously, and brought home a bottle of strong liquor to be used in case of sickness, and placed it conveniently in the shed, Mrs. Lane locked it up in the small chimney cupboard where she kept her camphor bottle and her opodeldoc and the other family medicines. She was not harsh with her husband. She cherished him tenderly, and worked diligently at her trade of tailoress, singing her hymns gayly in summer weather ; for she never had been so happy as now, when there was somebody to please beside herself, to cook for and sew for, and to live with and love. But Jerry complained more and more in his inmost heart that his wife expected too much of him. Presently he resumed an old habit of

resorting to the least respected of the two
country stores of that neighborhood, and sat
in the row of loafers on the outer steps.
" Sakes alive," said a shrewd observer one
day, " the fools set there and talk and talk
about what they went through when they
follered the sea, and when the women-folks
comes tradin' they are obleeged to climb
right over 'em."

Things grew worse and worse, until one
day Jerry Lane came home a little late to
dinner, and found his wife unusually grim-
faced and impatient. He took his seat
with an amiable smile, and showed in every
way a fine determination not to lose his temper because somebody else had. It was one
of the days when he looked almost boyish
and entirely irresponsible. His hair was
bright and curly from the dampness of the
east wind, and his wife was forced to remember how, in the days of their courtship, she
used to wish that she could pull one of the
curling locks straight, for the pleasure of
seeing it fly back. Nancy felt old and tired,
and was hurt in her very soul by the contrast between herself and her husband. " No
wonder I am aging, having to lug everything
on my shoulders," she thought. Jerry had

forgotten to do whatever she had asked him
for a day or two.   He had started out that
morning to go lobstering, but returned from
the direction of the village.

"Nancy," he said pleasantly, after he had
begun his dinner, a silent and solitary meal,
while his wife stitched busily by the window,
and refused to look at him, — " Nancy, I've
been thinking a good deal about a project."

"I hope it ain't going to cost so much
and bring in so little as your other notions
have, then," she responded quickly; though
somehow a memory of the hot day when
Jerry came and stood outside the fence, and
kissed her when it was settled he should stay
to supper, — a memory of that day would
keep fading and brightening in her mind.

"Yes," said Jerry humbly, "I ain't done
right, Nancy.   I ain't done my part for our
livin'.   I've let it sag right on to you, most
ever since we was married.   There was that
spell when I was kind of weakly, and had a
pain acrost me.   I tell you what it is: I
never was good for nothin' ashore, but now
I've got my strength up I'm going to show
ye what I can do.   I'm promised to ship
with Cap'n Low's brother, Skipper Nathan,
that sails out o' Eastport in the coasting

trade, lumber and so on. I shall get good wages, and you shall keep the whole on 't 'cept what I need for clothes."

" You need n't be so plaintive," said Ann in a sharp voice. " You can go if you want to. I have always been able to take care of myself, but when it comes to maintainin' two, 't ain't so easy. When be you goin'? "

" I expected you would be distressed," mourned Jerry, his face falling at this outbreak. " Nancy, you need n't be so quick. 'T ain't as if I had n't always set consid'able by ye, if I be wuthless."

Nancy's eyes flashed fire as she turned hastily away. Hardly knowing where she went, she passed through the open doorway, and crossed the clean green turf of the narrow side yard, and leaned over the garden fence. The young cabbages and cucumbers were nearly buried in weeds, and the currant bushes were fast being turned into skeletons by the ravaging worms. Jerry had forgotten to sprinkle them with hellebore, after all, though she had put the watering-pot into his very hand the evening before. She did not like to have the whole town laugh at her for hiring a man to do his work; she was busy from early morning

until late night, but she could not do everything herself.   She had been a fool to marry
this man, she told herself at last, and a sullen discontent and rage, that had been of
slow but certain growth, made her long to
free herself from this unprofitable hindrance
for a time, at any rate.   Go to sea?   Yes,
that was the best thing that could happen.
Perhaps when he had worked hard a while
on schooner fare, he would come home and
be good for something!

Jerry finished his dinner in the course of
time, and then sought his wife.   It was not
like her to go away in this silent fashion.
Of late her gift of speech had been proved
sufficiently formidable, and yet she had
never looked so resolutely angry as to-day.

"Nancy," he began, — "Nancy, girl!   I
ain't goin' off to leave you, if your heart's
set against it.   I'll spudge up and take
right holt."

But the wife turned slowly from the fence
and faced him.   Her eyes looked as if she
had been crying.   "You need n't stay on
my account," she said.   "I'll go right to
work an' fit ye out.   I'm sick of your
meechin' talk, and I don't want to hear no
more of it.   Ef *I* was a man" —

Jerry Lane looked crestfallen for a minute or two; but when his stern partner in life had disappeared within the house, he slunk away among the apple-trees of the little orchard, and sat down on the grass in a shady spot. It was getting to be warm weather, but he would go round and hoe the old girl's garden stuff by and by. There would be something going on aboard the schooner, and with delicious anticipation of future pleasure the delinquent Jerry struck his knee with his hand, as if he were clapping a crony on the shoulder. He also winked several times at the same fancied companion. Then, with a comfortable chuckle, he laid himself down, and pulled his old hat over his eyes, and went to sleep, while the weeds grew at their own sweet will, and the currant worms went looping and devouring from twig to twig.

III.

SUMMER went by, and winter began, and Mr. Jerry Lane did not reappear. He had promised to return in September when he parted from his wife early in June, for

Nancy had relented a little at the last, and sorrowed at the prospect of so long a separation. She had already learned the vacillations and uncertainties of her husband's character; but though she accepted the truth that her marriage had been in every way a piece of foolishness, she still clung affectionately to his assumed fondness for her. She could not believe that this marriage was only one of his makeshifts, and that as soon as he grew tired of the constraint he would be ready to throw the benefits of respectable home life to the four winds. A little sentimental speech-making and a few kisses the morning he went away, and the gratitude he might well have shown for her generous care-taking and provision for his voyage won her soft heart back again, and made poor, elderly, simple-hearted Nancy watch him cross the marshes with tears and foreboding. If she could have called him back that day, she would have done so and been thankful. And all summer and winter, whenever the wind blew and thrashed the drooping elm boughs against the low roof over her head, she was as full of fears and anxieties as if Jerry were her only son and making his first voyage at sea. The neigh-

bors pitied her for her disappointment.
They liked Nancy ; but they could not help
saying, " I told you so." It would have
been impossible not to respect the brave way
in which she met the world's eye, and carried herself with innocent unconsciousness
of having committed so laughable and unre-
warding a folly. The loafers on the store
steps had been unwontedly diverted one day,
when Jerry, who was their chief wit and
spokesman, rose slowly from his place, and
said in pious tones, " Boys, I must go this
minute. Grandma will keep dinner waiting." Mrs. Ann Lane did not show in her
aging face how young her heart was, and
after the schooner Susan Barnes had departed she seemed to pass swiftly from middle life and an almost youthful vigor to
early age and a look of spent strength and
dissatisfaction. " I suppose he did find it
stupid," she assured herself, with wistful
yearning for his rough words of praise,
when she sat down alone to her dinner, or
looked up sadly from her work, and missed
the amusing though unedifying conversation he was wont to offer on stormy winter
nights. How many of his marvelous tales
were true she never cared to ask. He had

come and gone, and she forgave him his shortcomings, and longed for his society with a heavy heart.

One spring day there was news in the Boston paper of the loss of the schooner Susan Barnes with all on board, and Nancy Lane's best friends shook their sage heads, and declared that as far as regarded that idle vagabond, Jerry Lane, it was all for the best. Nobody was interested in any other member of the crew, so the misfortune of the Susan Barnes seemed of but slight consequence in Walpole, she having passed out of her former owners' hands the autumn before. Jerry had stuck by the ship; at least, so he had sent word then to his wife by Skipper Nathan Low. The Susan Barnes was to sail regularly between Shediac and Newfoundland, and Jerry sent five dollars to Nancy, and promised to pay her a visit soon. "Tell her I'm layin' up somethin' handsome," he told the skipper with a grin, "and I've got some folks in Newfoundland I'll visit with on this voyage, and then I'll come ashore for good and farm it."

Mrs. Lane took the five dollars from the skipper as proudly as if Jerry had done the same thing so many times before that she

hardly noticed it. The skipper gave the
messages from Jerry, and felt that he had
done the proper thing. When the news
came long afterward that the schooner was
lost, that was the next thing that Nancy
knew about her wandering mate; and after
the minister had come solemnly to inform
her of her bereavement, and had gone away
again, and she sat down and looked her
widowhood in the face, there was not a sad-
der nor a lonelier woman in the town of
Walpole.

All the neighbors came to condole with
our heroine, and, though nobody was aware
of it, from that time she was really happier
and better satisfied with life than she had
ever been before. Now that she had an
ideal Jerry Lane to mourn over and think
about, to cherish and admire, she was day
by day slowly forgetting the trouble he had
been and the bitter shame of him, and ex-
alting his memory to something near saint-
liness. "He meant well," she told herself
again and again. She thought nobody could
tell so good a story; she felt that with her
own bustling, capable ways he had no chance
to do much that he might have done. She
had been too quick with him, and alas, alas!

how much better she would know how to
treat him if she could only see him again !
A sense of relief at his absence made her
continually assure herself of her great loss,
and, false even to herself, she mourned her
sometime lover diligently, and tried to think
herself a broken-hearted woman. It was
thought among those who knew Nancy Lane
best that she would recover her spirits in
time, but Jerry's wildest anticipations of a
proper respect to his memory were more
than realized in the first two years after the
schooner Susan Barnes went to the bottom
of the sea. His wife mourned for the man
he ought to have been, not for the real
Jerry, but she had loved him enough in the
beginning to make her own love a precious
possession for all time to come. It did not
matter much, after all, what manner of man
he was ; she had found in him something on
which to spend her hoarded affection.

IV.

NANCY LANE was a peaceable woman and
a good neighbor, but she never had been
able to get on with one fellow townswoman,

and that was Mrs. Deacon Elton. They managed to keep each other provoked and teased from one year's end to the other, and each good soul felt herself under a moral microscope, and understood that she was judged by a not very lenient criticism and discussion. Mrs. Lane clad herself in simple black after the news came of her husband's timely death, and Mrs. Elton made one of her farewell pilgrimages to church to see the new-made widow walk up the aisle.

"She need n't tell me she lays that afflic- tion so much to heart," the deacon's wife sniffed faintly, after her exhaustion had been met by proper treatment of camphor and a glass of currant wine, at the parson- age, where she rested a while after service. "Nancy Floyd knows she's well through with such a piece of nonsense. If I had had my health, I should have spoken with her and urged her not to take the step in the first place. She has n't spoken six beholden words to me since that vagabond come to Walpole. I dare say she may have heard something I said at the time she married. I declare for 't, I never was so outdone as when the deacon came home and informed me Nancy Floyd was going to be married.

She let herself down too low to ever hold
the place again that she used to hold in
folks' minds. And it's my opinion," said
the sharp-eyed little woman, " she ain't got
through with her pay yet."

But Mrs. Elton did not half comprehend
the unconscious prophecy with which her
words were freighted.

The months passed by : summer and winter came and went, and even those few persons who were misled by Nancy Lane's stern
visage and forbidding exterior into forgetting her kind heart were at last won over
to friendliness by her renewed devotion to
the sick and old people of the rural commu-
nity. She was so tender to little children
that they all loved her dearly. She was
ready to go to any household that needed
help, and in spite of her ceaseless industry
with her needle she found many a chance to
do good, and help her neighbors to lift and
carry the burdens of their lives. She blos-
somed out suddenly into a lovely, painstak-
ing eagerness to be of use ; it seemed as if
her affectionate heart, once made generous,
must go on spending its wealth wherever it
could find an excuse. Even Mrs. Elton her-

self was touched by her old enemy's evident wish to be friends, and said nothing more about poor Nancy's looking as savage as a hawk. The only thing to admit was the truth that her affliction had proved a blessing to her. And it was in a truly kind and compassionate spirit that, after hearing a shocking piece of news, the deacon's hysterical wife forbore to spread it far and wide through the town first, and went down to the Widow Lane's one September afternoon. Nancy was stitching busily upon the deacon's new coat, and looked up with a friendly smile as her guest came in, in spite of an instinctive shrug as she had seen her coming up the yard. The dislike of the poor souls for each other was deeper than their philosophy could reach.

Mrs. Elton spent some minutes in the unnecessary endeavor to regain her breath, and to her surprise found she must make a real effort before she could tell her unwelcome news. She had been so full of it all the way from home that she had rehearsed the whole interview; now she hardly knew how to begin. Nancy looked serener than usual, but there was something wistful about her face as she glanced across the room, presently, as if to understand the reason of the long pause. The clock ticked loudly; the kitten clattered a spool against the table-leg, and had begun to snarl the thread round her busy paws, and Nancy looked down and saw her; then the instant con-sciousness of there being some unhappy reason for Mrs. Elton's call made her forget the creature's mischief, and anxiously lay down her work to listen.

"Capt'in Nathan Low was to our house to dinner," the guest began. "He's bar-gaining with the deacon about some hay. He's got a new schooner, Capt'in Nathan has, and is going to build up a regular busi-ness of freighting hay to Boston by sea. There's no market to speak of about here, unless you haul it way over to Downer, and you can't make but one turn a day."

"'T would be a good thing," replied Nancy, trying to think that this was all, and perhaps the deacon wanted to hire her own field another year. He had underpaid her once, and they had not been on particu-larly good terms ever since. She would make her own bargains with Skipper Low, she thanked him and his wife!

"He's been down to the provinces these

two or three years back, you know," the
whining voice went on, and straightforward
Ann Lane felt the old animosity rising
within her. "At dinner-time I wa'n't able
to eat much of anything, and so I was talking with Capt'in Nathan, and asking him
some questions about them parts; and I
expressed something about the mercy 't was
his life should ha' been spared when that
schooner, the Susan Barnes, was lost so
quick after he sold out his part of her. And
I put in a word, bein' 's we were neighbors,
about how edifyin' your course had be'n
under affliction. I noticed then he 'd looked
sort o' queer whilst I was talkin', but there
was all the folks to the table, and you know
he 's a very cautious man, so he spoke of
somethin' else. 'T wa'n't half an hour after
dinner, I was comin' in with some plates
and cups, tryin' to help what my stren'th
would let me, and says he, 'Step out a little
ways into the piece with me, Mis' Elton. I
want to have a word with ye.' I went, too,
spite o' my neuralgy, for I saw he 'd got
somethin' on his mind. 'Look here,' says
he, 'I gathered from the way you spoke that
Jerry Lane's wife expects he 's dead.' Certain, says I, his name was in the list o' the

Susan Barnes's crew, and we read it in the paper. 'No,' says he to me, 'he ran away the day they sailed; he wa'n't aboard, and he's livin' with another woman down to Shediac.' Them was his very words."

Nancy Lane sank back in her chair, and covered her horror-stricken eyes with her hands. "'T ain't pleasant news to have to tell," Sister Elton went on mildly, yet with evident relish and full command of the occasion. "He said he seen Jerry the morning he came away. I thought you ought to know it. I'll tell you one thing, Nancy: I told the skipper to keep still about it, and now I've told you, I won't spread it no further to set folks a-talking. I'll keep it secret till you say the word. There ain't much trafficking betwixt here and there, and he's dead to you, certain, as much as if he laid up here in the burying-ground."

Nancy had bowed her head upon the table; the thin sandy hair was streaked with gray. She did not answer one word; this was the hardest blow of all.

"I'm much obliged to you for being so friendly," she said after a few minutes, looking straight before her now in a dazed sort of way, and lifting the new coat from the

floor, where it had fallen. " Yes, he 's dead
to me, — worse than dead, a good deal," and
her lip quivered. " I can't seem to bring
my thoughts to bear. I 've got so used to
thinkin' — No, don't you say nothin' to the
folks yet. I 'd do as much for you." And
Mrs. Elton knew that the smitten fellow-
creature before her spoke the truth, and
forebore.

Two or three days came and went, and
with every hour the quiet, simple-hearted
woman felt more grieved and unsteady in
mind and body. Such a shattering thunder-
bolt of news rarely falls into a human life.
She could not sleep ; she wandered to and
fro in the little house, and cried until she
could cry no longer. Then a great rage
spurred and excited her. She would go to
Shediac, and call Jerry Lane to account.
She would accuse him face to face ; and the
woman whom he was deceiving, as perhaps
he had deceived her, should know the base-
ness and cowardice of this miserable man.
So, dressed in her respectable Sunday
clothes, in the gray bonnet and shawl that
never had known any journeys except to
meeting, or to a country funeral or quiet

holiday-making, Nancy Lane trusted herself for the first time to the bewildering railway, to the temptations and dangers of the wide world outside the bounds of Walpole.

Two or three days later still, the quaint, thin figure familiar in Walpole highways flitted down the street of a provincial town. In the most primitive region of China this woman could hardly have felt a greater sense of foreign life and strangeness. At another time her native good sense and shrewd observation would have delighted in the experiences of this first week of travel, but she was too sternly angry and aggrieved, too deeply plunged in a survey of her own calamity, to take much notice of what was going on about her. Later she condemned the unworthy folly of the whole errand, but in these days the impulse to seek the culprit and confront him was irresistible.

The innkeeper's wife, a kindly creature, urged this puzzling guest to wait and rest and eat some supper, but Nancy refused, and without asking her way left the brightly lighted, flaring little public room, where curious eyes already offended her, and went out into the damp twilight. The voices of the street boys sounded outlandish, and she

felt more and more lonely. She longed for
Jerry to appear for protection's sake : she
forgot why she sought him, and was eager
to shelter herself behind the flimsy bulwark
of his manhood. She rebuked herself presently with terrible bitterness for a womanish
wonder whether he would say, " Why, Nancy,
girl ! " and be glad to see her. Poor woman,
it was a work-laden, serious girlhood that
had been hers, at any rate. The power of
giving her whole self in unselfish, enthusiastic, patient devotion had not belonged to her
youth only ; it had sprung fresh and blos-
soming in her heart as every new year came
and went.

One might have seen her stealing through
the shadows, skirting the edge of a lumber-
yard, stepping among the refuse of the harbor side, asking a question timidly now and
then of some passer-by. Yes, they knew
Jerry Lane, — his house was only a little
way off ; and one curious and compassionate
Scotchman, divining by some inner sense
the exciting nature of the errand, turned
back, and offered fruitlessly to go with the
stranger. " You know the man ? " he asked.
" He is his own enemy, but doing better
now that he is married. He minds his work,

I know that well; and he's taken a good wife." Nancy's heart beat faster with honest pride for a moment, until the shadow of the ugly truth and reality made it sink back to heaviness, and the fire of her smouldering rage was again kindled. She would speak to Jerry face to face before she slept, and a horrible contempt and scorn were ready for him, as with a glance either way along' the road she entered the narrow yard, and went noiselessly toward the window of a low, poor-looking house, from whence a bright light was shining out into the night.

Yes, there was Jerry, and it seemed as if she must faint and fall at the sight of him. How young he looked still! The thought smote her like a blow. They never were mates for each other, Jerry and she. Her own life was waning; she was an old woman.

He never had been so thrifty and respectable before; the other woman ought to know the savage truth about him, for all that! But at that moment the other woman stooped beside the supper table, and lifted a baby from its cradle, and put the dear, live little thing into its father's arms. The baby was wide-awake, and laughed at Jerry, who laughed back again, and it reached up to catch at a handful of the curly hair which had been poor Nancy's delight.

The other woman stood there looking at them, full of pride and love. She was young, and trig, and neat. She looked a brisk, efficient little creature. Perhaps Jerry would make something of himself now; he always had it in him. The tears were running down Nancy's cheeks; the rain, too, had begun to fall. She stood there watching the little household sit down to supper, and noticed with eager envy how well cooked the food was, and how hungrily the master of the house ate what was put before him. All thoughts of ending the new wife's sin and folly vanished away. She could not enter in and break another heart; hers was broken already, and it would not matter. And Nancy Lane, a widow indeed, crept away again, as silently as she had come, to think what was best to be done, to find alternate woe and comfort in the memory of the sight she had seen.

The little house at the edge of the Walpole marshes seemed full of blessed shelter and comfort the evening that its forsaken mistress came back to it. Her strength was

spent; she felt much more desolate now that
she had seen with her own eyes that Jerry
Lane was alive than when she had counted
him among the dead. An uncharacteristic
disregard of the laws of the land filled this
good woman's mind. Jerry had his life to
live, and she wished him no harm. She
wondered often how the baby grew, and
fancied again and again the changes and
conditions of the far-away household. Alas!
she knew only too well the weakness of the
man, and once she exclaimed, in a grim out-
burst of impatience, " I 'd rather others
should have to cope with him than me ! "

But that evening, when she came back
from Shediac, and sat in the dark for a
long time, lest Mrs. Elton should see the
light and risk her life in the evening air to
bring unwelcome sympathy, — that evening,
I say, came the hardest moment of all, when
Ann Floyd, tailoress, of so many virtuous,
self-respecting years, whose idol had turned
to clay, who was shamed, disgraced, and
wronged, sat down alone to supper in the
little kitchen.

She had put one cup and saucer on the
table and then stood and looked at them
through bitter tears. Somehow a conscious-

ness of her solitary age, her uncompanioned future, rushed through her mind; the failure of her best earthly hope was enough to break a stronger woman's heart.

Who can laugh at my Marsh Rosemary, or who can cry, for that matter? The gray primness of the plant is made up from a hundred colors if you look close enough to find them. This Marsh Rosemary stands in her own place, and holds her dry leaves and tiny blossoms steadily toward the same sun that the pink lotus blooms for, and the white rose.

A WHITE HERON.

I.

THE woods were already filled with shadows one June evening, just before eight o'clock, though a bright sunset still glimmered faintly among the trunks of the trees. A little girl was driving home her cow, a plodding, dilatory, provoking creature in her behavior, but a valued companion for all that. They were going away from the western light, and striking deep into the dark woods, but their feet were familiar with the path, and it was no matter whether their eyes could see it or not.

There was hardly a night the summer through when the old cow could be found waiting at the pasture bars; on the contrary, it was her greatest pleasure to hide herself away among the high huckleberry bushes, and though she wore a loud bell she had made the discovery that if one stood per-

fectly still it would not ring. So Sylvia had
to hunt for her until she found her, and call
Co'! Co'! with never an answering Moo,
until her childish patience was quite spent.
If the creature had not given good milk and
plenty of it, the case would have seemed
very different to her owners. Besides, Sylvia had all the time there was, and very
little use to make of it. Sometimes in pleasant weather it was a consolation to look
upon the cow's pranks as an intelligent at-
tempt to play hide and seek, and as the child
had no playmates she lent herself to this
amusement with a good deal of zest. Though
this chase had been so long that the wary
animal herself had given an unusual signal
of her whereabouts, Sylvia had only laughed
when she came upon Mistress Moolly at the
swamp-side, and urged her affectionately
homeward with a twig of birch leaves. The
old cow was not inclined to wander farther,
she even turned in the right direction for
once as they left the pasture, and stepped
along the road at a good pace. She was
quite ready to be milked now, and seldom
stopped to browse. Sylvia wondered what
her grandmother would say because they
were so late. It was a great while since she

had left home at half past five o'clock, but
everybody knew the difficulty of making this
errand a short one. Mrs. Tilley had chased
the hornéd torment too many summer even-
ings herself to blame any one else for lingering, and was only thankful as she waited
that she had Sylvia, nowadays, to give such
valuable assistance. The good woman suspected that Sylvia loitered occasionally on
her own account; there never was such a
child for straying about out-of-doors since
the world was made! Everybody said that it
was a good change for a little maid who had
tried to grow for eight years in a crowded
manufacturing town, but, as for Sylvia herself, it seemed as if she never had been alive
at all before she came to live at the farm.
She thought often with wistful compassion
of a wretched dry geranium that belonged
to a town neighbor.

"'Afraid of folks,'" old Mrs. Tilley said
to herself, with a smile, after she had made
the unlikely choice of Sylvia from her
daughter's houseful of children, and was returning to the farm. "'Afraid of folks,'
they said! I guess she won't be troubled
no great with 'em up to the old place!"
When they reached the door of the lonely

house and stopped to unlock it, and the cat
came to purr loudly, and rub against them,
a deserted pussy, indeed, but fat with young
robins, Sylvia whispered that this was a
beautiful place to live in, and she never
should wish to go home.

The companions followed the shady wood-
road, the cow taking slow steps, and the
child very fast ones. The cow stopped long
at the brook to drink, as if the pasture were
not half a swamp, and Sylvia stood still and
waited, letting her bare feet cool themselves
in the shoal water, while the great twilight
moths struck softly against her. She waded
on through the brook as the cow moved
away, and listened to the thrushes with a
heart that beat fast with pleasure. There
was a stirring in the great boughs overhead.
They were full of little birds and beasts that
seemed to be wide-awake, and going about
their world, or else saying good-night to
each other in sleepy twitters. Sylvia herself
felt sleepy as she walked along. However,
it was not much farther to the house, and
the air was soft and sweet. She was not
often in the woods so late as this, and it
made her feel as if she were a part of the

gray shadows and the moving leaves. She
was just thinking how long it seemed since
she first came to the farm a year ago, and
wondering if everything went on in the
noisy town just the same as when she was
there; the thought of the great red-faced
boy who used to chase and frighten her made
her hurry along the path to escape from the
shadow of the trees.

Suddenly this little woods-girl is horror-
stricken to hear a clear whistle not very far
away. Not a bird's whistle, which would
have a sort of friendliness, but a boy's whistle, determined, and somewhat aggressive.
Sylvia left the cow to whatever sad fate
might await her, and stepped discreetly aside
into the bushes, but she was just too late.
The enemy had discovered her, and called
out in a very cheerful and persuasive tone,
"Halloa, little girl, how far is it to the
road?" and trembling Sylvia answered almost inaudibly, "A good ways."

She did not dare to look boldly at the tall
young man, who carried a gun over his
shoulder, but she came out of her bush and
again followed the cow, while he walked
alongside.

"I have been hunting for some birds,"

the stranger said kindly, " and I have lost
my way, and need a friend very much.
Don't be afraid," he added gallantly. "Speak
up and tell me what your name is, and
whether you think I can spend the night at
your house, and go out gunning early in the
morning."

Sylvia was more alarmed than before.
Would not her grandmother consider her
much to blame? But who could have fore-
seen such an accident as this? It did not appear to be her fault, and she hung her head
as if the stem of it were broken, but managed to answer "Sylvy," with much effort
when her companion again asked her name.

Mrs. Tilley was standing in the doorway
when the trio came into view. The cow
gave a loud moo by way of explanation.

" Yes, you'd better speak up for yourself,
you old trial! Where 'd she tucked herself
away this time, Sylvy?" Sylvia kept an
awed silence; she knew by instinct that her
grandmother did not comprehend the gravity of the situation. She must be mistaking
the stranger for one of the farmer-lads of
the region.

The young man stood his gun beside the
door, and dropped a heavy game-bag beside

it; then he bade Mrs. Tilley good-evening, and repeated his wayfarer's story, and asked if he could have a night's lodging.

" Put me anywhere you like," he said. " I must be off early in the morning, before day; but I am very hungry, indeed. You can give me some milk at any rate, that's plain."

" Dear sakes, yes," responded the hostess, whose long slumbering hospitality seemed to be easily awakened. " You might fare better if you went out on the main road a mile or so, but you're welcome to what we've got. I'll milk right off, and you make yourself at home. You can sleep on husks or feathers," she proffered graciously. " I raised them all myself. There's good pasturing for geese just below here towards the ma'sh. Now step round and set a plate for the gentleman, Sylvy!" And Sylvia promptly stepped. She was glad to have something to do, and she was hungry herself.

It was a surprise to find so clean and comfortable a little dwelling in this New England wilderness. The young man had known the horrors of its most primitive housekeeping, and the dreary squalor of that level of society which does not rebel at the companionship of hens. This was the best thrift of an old-fashioned farmstead, though on such a small scale that it seemed like a hermitage. He listened eagerly to the old woman's quaint talk, he watched Sylvia's pale face and shining gray eyes with ever growing enthusiasm, and insisted that this was the best supper he had eaten for a month; then, afterward, the new - made friends sat down in the doorway together while the moon came up.

Soon it would be berry-time, and Sylvia was a great help at picking. The cow was a good milker, though a plaguy thing to keep track of, the hostess gossiped frankly, adding presently that she had buried four children, so that Sylvia's mother, and a son (who might be dead) in California were all the children she had left. "Dan, my boy, was a great hand to go gunning," she explained sadly. "I never wanted for pa'tridges or gray squer'ls while he was to home. He 's been a great wand'rer, I expect, and he 's no hand to write letters. There, I don't blame him, I 'd ha' seen the world myself if it had been so I could.

"Sylvia takes after him," the grand-

mother continued affectionately, after a minute's pause. " There ain't a foot o' ground
she don't know her way over, and the wild
creatur's counts her one o' themselves.
Squer'ls she'll tame to come an' feed right
out o' her hands, and all sorts o' birds. Last
winter she got the jay-birds to bangeing
here, and I believe she'd 'a' scanted herself
of her own meals to have plenty to throw
out amongst 'em, if I had n't kep' watch.
Anything but crows, I tell her, I'm willin'
to help support, — though Dan he went an'
tamed one o' them that did seem to have
reason same as folks. It was round here
a good spell after he went away. Dan an'
his father they did n't hitch, — but he never
held up his head ag'in after Dan had dared
him an' gone off."

The guest did not notice this hint of family sorrows in his eager interest in something else.

" So Sylvy knows all about birds, does
she ? " he exclaimed, as he looked round at
the little girl who sat, very demure but increasingly sleepy, in the moonlight. " I am
making a collection of birds myself. I have
been at it ever since I was a boy." (Mrs.
Tilley smiled.) " There are two or three

very rare ones I have been hunting for these five years. I mean to get them on my own ground if they can be found."

" Do you cage 'em up ? " asked Mrs. Tilley doubtfully, in response to this enthusiastic announcement.

" Oh, no, they 're stuffed and preserved, dozens and dozens of them," said the ornithologist, " and I have shot or snared every one myself. I caught a glimpse of a white heron three miles from here on Saturday, and I have followed it in this direction. They have never been found in this district at all. The little white heron, it is," and he turned again to look at Sylvia with the hope of discovering that the rare bird was one of her acquaintances.

But Sylvia was watching a hop-toad in the narrow footpath.

" You would know the heron if you saw it," the stranger continued eagerly. " A queer tall white bird with soft feathers and long thin legs. And it would have a nest perhaps in the top of a high tree, made of sticks, something like a hawk's nest."

Sylvia's heart gave a wild beat; she knew that strange white bird, and had once stolen softly near where it stood in some bright green swamp grass, away over at the other side of the woods. There was an open place where the sunshine always seemed strangely yellow and hot, where tall, nodding rushes grew, and her grandmother had warned her that she might sink in the soft black mud underneath and never be heard of more. Not far beyond were the salt marshes and beyond those was the sea, the sea which Sylvia wondered and dreamed about, but never had looked upon, though its great voice could often be heard above the noise of the woods on stormy nights.

"I can't think of anything I should like so much as to find that heron's nest," the handsome stranger was saying. "I would give ten dollars to anybody who could show it to me," he added desperately, "and I mean to spend my whole vacation hunting for it if need be. Perhaps it was only migrating, or had been chased out of its own region by some bird of prey."

Mrs. Tilley gave amazed attention to all this, but Sylvia still watched the toad, not divining, as she might have done at some calmer time, that the creature wished to get to its hole under the doorstep, and was much hindered by the unusual spectators at that hour of the evening. No amount of thought, that night, could decide how many wished-for treasures the ten dollars, so lightly spoken of, would buy.

The next day the young sportsman hovered about the woods, and Sylvia kept him company, having lost her first fear of the friendly lad, who proved to be most kind and sympathetic. He told her many things about the birds and what they knew and where they lived and what they did with themselves. And he gave her a jack-knife, which she thought as great a treasure as if she were a desert-islander. All day long he did not once make her troubled or afraid except when he brought down some unsuspecting singing creature from its bough. Sylvia would have liked him vastly better without his gun; she could not understand why he killed the very birds he seemed to like so much. But as the day waned, Sylvia still watched the young man with loving admiration. She had never seen anybody so charming and delightful; the woman's heart, asleep in the child, was vaguely thrilled by a dream of love. Some premonition of that great power stirred and swayed these young

foresters who traversed the solemn woodlands with soft-footed silent care. They
stopped to listen to a bird's song; they
pressed forward again eagerly, parting the
branches, — speaking to each other rarely
and in whispers; the young man going first
and Sylvia following, fascinated, a few steps
behind, with her gray eyes dark with excitement.

She grieved because the longed-for white
heron was elusive, but she did not lead the
guest, she only followed, and there was no
such thing as speaking first. The sound of
her own unquestioned voice would have ter-
rified her, — it was hard enough to answer
yes or no when there was need of that. At
last evening began to fall, and they drove
the cow home together, and Sylvia smiled
with pleasure when they came to the place
where she heard the whistle and was afraid
only the night before.

II.

HALF a mile from home, at the farther
edge of the woods, where the land was high-
est, a great pine-tree stood, the last of its

generation. Whether it was left for a boundary mark, or for what reason, no one could say; the woodchoppers who had felled its mates were dead and gone long ago, and a whole forest of sturdy trees, pines and oaks and maples, had grown again. But the stately head of this old pine towered above them all and made a landmark for sea and shore miles and miles away. Sylvia knew it well. She had always believed that whoever climbed to the top of it could see the ocean; and the little girl had often laid her hand on the great rough trunk and looked up wistfully at those dark boughs that the wind always stirred, no matter how hot and still the air might be below. Now she thought of the tree with a new excitement, for why, if one climbed it at break of day, could not one see all the world, and easily discover whence the white heron flew, and mark the place, and find the hidden nest?

What a spirit of adventure, what wild ambition! What fancied triumph and delight and glory for the later morning when she could make known the secret! It was almost too real and too great for the childish heart to bear.

All night the door of the little house

stood open, and the whippoorwills came and sang upon the very step. The young sportsman and his old hostess were sound asleep, but Sylvia's great design kept her broad awake and watching. She forgot to think of sleep. The short summer night seemed as long as the winter darkness, and at last when the whippoorwills ceased, and she was afraid the morning would after all come too soon, she stole out of the house and followed the pasture path through the woods, hastening toward the open ground beyond, listening with a sense of comfort and companionship to the drowsy twitter of a half-awakened bird, whose perch she had jarred in passing. Alas, if the great wave of human interest which flooded for the first time this dull little life should sweep away the satisfactions of an existence heart to heart with nature and the dumb life of the forest!

There was the huge tree asleep yet in the paling moonlight, and small and hopeful Sylvia began with utmost bravery to mount to the top of it, with tingling, eager blood coursing the channels of her whole frame, with her bare feet and fingers, that pinched and held like bird's claws to the monstrous ladder reaching up, up, almost to the sky itself.

First she must mount the white oak tree that grew alongside, where she was almost lost among the dark branches and the green leaves heavy and wet with dew; a bird fluttered off its nest, and a red squirrel ran to and fro and scolded pettishly at the harmless housebreaker. Sylvia felt her way easily. She had often climbed there, and knew that higher still one of the oak's upper branches chafed against the pine trunk, just where its lower boughs were set close together. There, when she made the dangerous pass from one tree to the other, the great enterprise would really begin.

She crept out along the swaying oak limb at last, and took the daring step across into the old pine-tree. The way was harder than she thought; she must reach far and hold fast, the sharp dry twigs caught and held her and scratched her like angry talons, the pitch made her thin little fingers clumsy and stiff as she went round and round the tree's great stem, higher and higher upward. The sparrows and robins in the woods below were beginning to wake and twitter to the dawn, yet it seemed much lighter there aloft in the pine-tree, and the child knew that she must hurry if her project were to be of any use.

The tree seemed to lengthen itself out as she went up, and to reach farther and farther upward. It was like a great main-mast to the voyaging earth; it must truly have been amazed that morning through all its ponderous frame as it felt this determined spark of human spirit creeping and climbing from higher branch to branch. Who knows how steadily the least twigs held themselves to advantage this light, weak creature on her way! The old pine must have loved his new dependent. More than all the hawks, and bats, and moths, and even the sweet - voiced thrushes, was the brave, beating heart of the solitary gray-eyed child. And the tree stood still and held away the winds that June morning while the dawn grew bright in the east.

Sylvia's face was like a pale star, if one had seen it from the ground, when the last thorny bough was past, and she stood trembling and tired but wholly triumphant, high in the tree-top. Yes, there was the sea with the dawning sun making a golden dazzle over it, and toward that glorious east flew two hawks with slow-moving pinions. How low they looked in the air from that height when before one had only seen them far up,

and dark against the blue sky. Their gray
feathers were as soft as moths; they seemed
only a little way from the tree, and Sylvia
felt as if she too could go flying away among
the clouds. Westward, the woodlands and
farms reached miles and miles into the distance; here and there were church steeples,
and white villages; truly it was a vast and
awesome world.

The birds sang louder and louder. At
last the sun came up bewilderingly bright.
Sylvia could see the white sails of ships out
at sea, and the clouds that were purple and
rose-colored and yellow at first began to fade
away. Where was the white heron's nest in
the sea of green branches, and was this wonderful sight and pageant of the world the
only reward for having climbed to such a
giddy height? Now look down again, Sylvia, where the green marsh is set among the
shining birches and dark hemlocks; there
where you saw the white heron once you will
see him again; look, look! a white spot of
him like a single floating feather comes up
from the dead hemlock and grows larger,
and rises, and comes close at last, and goes
by the landmark pine with steady sweep of
wing and outstretched slender neck and

crested head. And wait! wait! do not
move a foot or a finger, little girl, do not
send an arrow of light and consciousness
from your two eager eyes, for the heron has
perched on a pine bough not far beyond
yours, and cries back to his mate on the
nest, and plumes his feathers for the new
day!

The child gives a long sigh a minute
later when a company of shouting cat-birds
comes also to the tree, and vexed by their
fluttering and lawlessness the solemn heron
goes away. She knows his secret now, the
wild, light, slender bird that floats and wa-
vers, and goes back like an arrow presently
to his home in the green world beneath.
Then Sylvia, well satisfied, makes her peril-
ous way down again, not daring to look far
below the branch she stands on, ready to cry
sometimes because her fingers ache and her
lamed feet slip. Wondering over and over
again what the stranger would say to her,
and what he would think when she told him
how to find his way straight to the heron's
nest.

"Sylvy, Sylvy!" called the busy old
grandmother again and again, but nobody

answered, and the small husk bed was empty, and Sylvia had disappeared.

The guest waked from a dream, and remembering his day's pleasure hurried to dress himself that it might sooner begin. He was sure from the way the shy little girl looked once or twice yesterday that she had at least seen the white heron, and now she must really be persuaded to tell. Here she comes now, paler than ever, and her worn old frock is torn and tattered, and smeared with pine pitch. The grandmother and the sportsman stand in the door together and question her, and the splendid moment has come to speak of the dead hemlock-tree by the green marsh.

But Sylvia does not speak after all, though the old grandmother fretfully rebukes her, and the young man's kind appealing eyes are looking straight in her own. He can make them rich with money; he has promised it, and they are poor now. He is so well worth making happy, and he waits to hear the story she can tell.

No, she must keep silence! What is it that suddenly forbids her and makes her dumb? Has she been nine years growing, and now, when the great world for the first

time puts out a hand to her, must she thrust
it aside for a bird's sake? The murmur of
the pine's green branches is in her ears, she
remembers how the white heron came flying
through the golden air and how they watched
the sea and the morning together, and Sylvia cannot speak; she cannot tell the heron's
secret and give its life away.

Dear loyalty, that suffered a sharp pang
as the guest went away disappointed later in
the day, that could have served and followed
him and loved him as a dog loves! Many
a night Sylvia heard the echo of his whistle
haunting the pasture path as she came home
with the loitering cow. She forgot even her
sorrow at the sharp report of his gun and
the piteous sight of thrushes and sparrows
dropping silent to the ground, their songs
hushed and their pretty feathers stained and
wet with blood. Were the birds better
friends than their hunter might have been,
— who can tell? Whatever treasures were
lost to her, woodlands and summer-time, remember! Bring your gifts and graces and
tell your secrets to this lonely country child!

LAW LANE.

I.

THE thump of a flat-iron signified to an educated passer-by that this was Tuesday morning; yesterday having been fair and the weekly washing-day unhindered by the weather. It was undoubtedly what Mrs. Powder pleased herself by calling a good orthodox week; not one of the disjointed and imperfect sections of time which a rainy Monday forced upon methodical housekeepers. Mrs. Powder was not a woman who could live altogether in the present, and whatever she did was done with a view to having it cleared out of the way of the next enterprise on her list. "I can't bear to see folks do their work as if every piece on 't was a tread-mill," she used to say, briskly. "Life means progriss to me, and I can't dwell by the way no more 'n sparks can fly downwards. 'T ain't the way I 'm built, nor none of the Fisher tribe."

The hard white bundles in the shallow splint-basket were disappearing, one by one, and taking their places on the decrepit clothes-horse, well ironed and precisely folded. The July sunshine came in at one side of Mrs. Powder's kitchen, and the cool northwest breeze blew the heat out again from the other side. Mrs. Powder grew uneasy and impatient as she neared the end of her task, and the flat-iron moved more and more vigorously. She kept glancing out through the doorway and along the country road as if she were watching for somebody.

"I shall just have to git ready an' go an' rout her out myself, an' take my chances," she said at last with a resentful look at the clock, as if it were partly to blame for the delay and had ears with which to listen to proper rebuke. The round moon-face had long ago ceased its waxing and waning across the upper part of the old dial, as if it had forgotten its responsibility about the movements of a heavenly body in its pleased concern about housekeeping.

"See here!" said Mrs. Powder, taking a last hot iron from the fire. "You ain't a-keepin' time like you used to; you 're gettin' lazy, I must say. Look at this 'ere sun-mark on the floor, that calls it full 'leven o'clock, and you want six minutes to ten. I 've got to send word to the clock-man and have your in'ards all took apart; you got me to meetin' more 'n half an hour too late, Sabbath last."

To which the moon-face did not change its beaming expression ; very likely, being a moon, it was not willing to mind the ways of the sun.

"Lord, what an old thing you be!" said Mrs. Powder, turning away with a chuckle. "I don't wonder your sense kind of fails you!" And the clock clucked at her by way of answer, though presently it was going to strike ten at any rate.

The hot iron was now put down hurriedly, and the half-ironed night-cap was left in a queer position on the ironing-board. A small figure had appeared in the road and was coming toward the house with a fleet, barefooted run which required speedy action. "Here you, Joel Smith!" shouted the old woman. "Jo—el!" But the saucy lad only doubled his pace and pretended not to see or hear her. Mrs. Powder could play at that game, too, and did not call again, but quietly went back to her ironing and tried as hard as she could to be provoked. Presently the boy came panting up the slope of green turf which led from the road to the kitchen doorstep.

"I didn't know but you spoke as I ran by," he remarked, in an amiable tone. Mrs. Powder took no heed of him whatever.

"I ain't in no hurry; I kind o' got running," he explained, a moment later; and then, as his hostess stepped toward the stove, he caught up the frilled night-cap and tied it on in a twinkling. When Mrs. Powder turned again, the sight of him was too much for her gravity.

"Them frills is real becoming to ye," she announced, shaking with laughter. "I declare for 't if you don't favor your gran'ma Dodge's looks. I should like to have yer folks see ye. There, take it off now; I'm most through my ironin' and I want to clear it out o' the way."

Joel was perfectly docile and laid the night-cap within reach. He had a temptation to twitch it back by the end of one string, but he refrained. "Want me to go drive your old brown hen-turkey out o' the wet grass, Mis' Powder? She's tolling her chicks off down to'a'ds the swamp," he offered.

"She's raised up families enough to know how by this time," said Mrs. Powder, "an' the swamp's dry as a bone."

"I'll split ye up a mess o' kindlin'-wood whilst I'm here, jest as soon's not," said Joel, in a still more pleasant tone, after a long and anxious pause.

"There, I'll get ye your doughnuts, pretty quick. They ain't so fresh as they was Saturday. I s'pose that's what you're driving at." The good soul shook with laughter. Joel answered as well for her amusement as the most famous of comic actors; there was something in his appealing eyes, his thin cheeks and monstrous freckles, and his long locks of sandy hair, which was very funny to Mrs. Powder. She was always interested, too, in fruitless attempts to satisfy his appetite. He listened now, for the twentieth time, to her opinion that the bottomless pit alone could be compared to the recesses of his being. "I should like to be able to say that I had filled ye up jest once!" she ended her remarks, as she brought a tin pan full of doughnuts from her pantry.

"Heard the news?" asked small Joel, as he viewed the provisions with glistening eyes. He bore likeness to a little hungry woodchuck, or muskrat, as he went to work before the tin pan.

" What news ? " Mrs. Powder asked, suspiciously. " I ain't seen nobody this day."

"Barnet's folks has got their case in court."

" They ain't ! " and while a solemn silence fell upon the kitchen, the belated old clock whirred and rumbled and struck ten with persistent effort. Mrs. Powder looked round at it impatiently ; the moon-face confronted her with the same placid smile.

" Twelve o'clock's the time you git your dinner, ain't it, Mis' Powder ? " the boy inquired, as if he had repeated his news like a parrot and had no further interest in its meaning.

" I don't plot for to get me no reg'lar dinner this day," was the unexpected reply. " You can eat a couple or three o' them nuts and step along, for all I care. An' I want you to go up Lyddy Bangs's lane and carry her word that I'm goin' out to pick me some blueberries. They'll be ripened up elegant, and I've got a longin' for 'em. Tell her I say 't is our day — she'll know ; we've be'n after 'arly blueberries together this forty years, and Lyddy knows where to meet with me; there by them split rocks."

The ironing was finished a few minutes afterward, and the board was taken to its place in the shed. When Mrs. Powder returned, Joel had stealthily departed; the tin pan was turned upside down on the seat of the kitchen chair. " Good land! " said the astonished woman, " I believe he'll bu'st himself to everlastin' bliss one o' these days. Them doughnuts would have lasted me till Thursday, certain."

"Gimme suthin' to eat, Mis' Powder?" whined Joel at the window, with his plaintive countenance lifted just above the sill. But he set forth immediately down the road, with bulging pockets and the speed of a light-horseman.

II.

Half an hour later the little gray farmhouse was shut and locked, and its mistress was crossing the next pasture with a surprisingly quick step for a person of her age and weight. An old cat was trotting after her, with tail high in the air, but it was plain to see that she still looked for danger, having just come down from the woodpile, where she had retreated on Joel's first approach. She kept as close to Mrs. Powder as was consistent with short excursions after crickets or young, unwary sparrows, and opened her wide green eyes fearfully on the lookout for that evil monster, the boy.

There were two pastures to cross, and Mrs. Powder was very much heated by the noonday sun and entirely out of breath when she approached the familiar rendezvous and caught sight of her friend's cape-bonnet.

"Ain't there no justice left?" was her indignant salutation. "I s'pose you've heard that Crosby's folks have lost their case? Poor Mis' Crosby! 't will kill her, I'm sure. I've be'n calculatin' to go berryin' all the forenoon, but I couldn't git word to you till Joel came tootin' by. I thought likely you'd expect notice when you see what a good day 't was."

"I did," replied Lyddy Bangs, in a tone much more serious than her companion's. She was a thin, despairing little body, with an anxious face and a general look of disappointment and poverty, though really the more prosperous person of the two. "Joel

told me you said 't was our day," she added.
" I 'm wore out tryin' to satisfy that boy;
he 's always beggin' for somethin' to eat
every time he comes nigh the house. I
should think they 'd see to him to home;
not let him batten on the neighbors so."

" You ain't been feedin' of him, too ?"
laughed Mrs. Powder. " Well, I declare, I
don't see whar he puts it ! " and she fanned
herself with her apron. " I always forget
what a sightly spot this is."

" Here 's your pussy - cat, ain't she ?"
asked Lyddy Bangs, needlessly, as they sat
looking off over the valley. Behind them
the hills rose one above another, with their
bare upland clearings and great stretches of
pine and beech forest. Beyond the wide
valley was another range of hills, green and
pleasant in the clear mid-day light. Some
higher mountains loomed, sterile and stony,
to northward. They were on the women's
right as they sat looking westward.

" It does seem as if folks might keep the
peace when the Lord's give 'em so pooty a
a spot to live in," said Lyddy Bangs, re-
gretfully. " There ain't no better farms
than Barnet's and Crosby's folks have got
neither, but 'stead o' neighboring they must

pick their mean fusses and fight from generation to generation. My gran'ma'am used to say 't was just so with 'em when she was a girl — and she was one of the first settlers up this way. She al'ays would have it that Barnet's folks was the most to blame, but there 's plenty sides with 'em, as you know."

"There, 't is all mixed up, so 't is — a real tangle," answered Mrs. Powder. "I 've been o' both minds — I must say I used to hold for the Crosbys in the old folks' time, but I 've come round to see they ain't perfect. There! I 'm b'ilin' over with somethin' I 've got to tell somebody. I 've kep' it close long 's I can."

"Let 's get right to pickin', then," said Lyddy Bangs, "or we sha'n't budge from here the whole livin' afternoon," and the small thin figure and the tall stout one moved off together toward their well-known harvest-fields. They were presently settled down within good hearing distance, and yet the discussion was not begun. The cat curled herself for a nap on the smooth top of a rock.

"There, I have to eat a while first, like a young-one," said Mrs. Powder. "I always tell 'em that blueberries is only fit to eat

right off of the twigs. You want 'em full o'
sun; let 'em git cold and they 're only fit to
cook — not but what I eat 'em any ways
I can git 'em. Ain't they nice an' spicy?
Law, my poor knees is so stiff! I begin to
be afraid, nowadays, every year o' berryin'
may be my last. I don' know why 't should
be that my knees serves me so. I ain't
rheumaticky, nor none o' my folks was; we
go off with other complaints."

"The mukis membrane o' the knees gits
dried up," explained Lyddy Bangs, "an'
the j'ints is all powder-posted. So I 've be'n
told, anyways."

"Then they was ignorant," retorted her
companion, sharply. "I know by the feelin's
I have" — and the two friends picked in-
dustriously and discussed the vexed points
of medicine no more.

"I can't force them Barnets and Crosbys out o' my mind," suggested Miss Bangs
after a while, being eager to receive the
proffered confidence which might be forgotten. "Think of 'em, without no other
door-neighbors, fightin' for three ginerations
over the bounds of a lane wall. What if
't was two foot one way or two foot t'other,
let 'em agree."

" But that's just what they could n't,"
said Mrs. Powder. "You know yourself
you might be willin' to give away a piece o'
land, but when somebody said 't wa'n't yours,
't was theirs, 't would take more Christian
grace 'n I 've got to let 'em see I thought they
was right. All the old Crosbys ever wanted,
first, was for the Barnets to say two foot of
the lane was theirs by rights, and then they
was willin' to turn it into the lane and to
give that two foot more o' the wedth than
Barnets did — they wa'n't haggling for no
pay; 't was for rights. But Barnet's folks
said " —

"Now, don't you go an' git all flustered
up a-tellin' that over, Harri't Powder," said
the lesser woman. "There ain't be'n no
words spoke so often as them along this
sidelin' hill, not even the Ten Command-
ments. The only sense there's be'n about
it is, they 've let each other alone altogether,
and ain't spoke at all for six months to a
time. I can't help hoping that the war 'll
die out with the old breed and they 'll come
to some sort of peace. Mis' Barnet was a
Sands, and they 're toppin' sort o' folks and
she 's got fight in her. I think she 's more
to blame than Barnet, a good sight; but

Mis' Crosby 's a downright peace-making little creatur', and would have ended it long
ago if she 'd be'n able."

"Barnet's stubborn, too, let me tell you!"
and Mrs. Powder's voice was full of anger.
"'T will never die out in his day, and he 'll
spend every cent lawing, as the old folks
did afore him. The lawyers must laugh at
him well, 'mongst themselves. One an' another o' the best on 'em has counseled them
to leave it out to referees, and tried to show
'em they was fools. My man talked with
judge himself about it, once, after he 'd been
settin' on a jury and they was comin' away
from court. They could n't agree; they
never could! All the spare money o' both
farms has gone to pay the lawyers and carry
on one fight after another. Now folks don't
know it, but Crosby's farm is all mortgaged; they 've spent even what Mis' Crosby
had from her folks. An' there 's worse behind — there 's worse behind," insisted the
speaker, stoutly. "I went up there this
spring, as you know, when Mis' Crosby was
at death's door with lung-fever. I went
through everything fetchin' of her round,
and was there five weeks, till she got about.
'I feel to'a'ds you as an own sister,' says

Abby Crosby to me. ' I 'm a neighboring
woman at heart,' says she; 'and just you
think of it, that my man had to leave me
alone, sick as I was, while he went for you
and the doctor, not riskin' to ask Barnet's
folks to send for help. I like to live pleasant,' says she to me, and bu'st right out
a-cryin'. I knew then how she 'd felt things
all these years. — How are they ever goin'
to pay more court bills and all them piles o'
damages, if the farm 's mortgaged so heavy?"
she resumed. "Crosby's farm ain't worth
a good two thirds of Barnet's. They 've
both neglected their lands. How many you
got so fur, Lyddy?"

Lyddy proudly displayed her gains of
blueberries; the pail was filling very fast,
and the friends were at their usual game of
rivalry. Mrs. Powder had been the faster
picker in years past, and she now doubled
her diligence.

"Ain't the sweet-fern thick an' scented
as ever you see?" she said. "Gimme pas-
ture-lands rather 'n the best gardins that
grows. If I can have a sweet-brier bush
and sweet-fern patch and some clumps o'
bayberry, you can take all the gardin blooms.
Look how folks toils with witch-grass and

pusley and gets a starved lot o' poor sprigs,
slug-eat, and all dyin' together in their front
yards, when they might get better comfort
in the first pasture along the road. I guess
there's somethin' wild, that's never got
tutored out o' me. I must ha' be'n made
o' somethin' counter to town dust. I never
could see why folks wanted to go off an'
live out o' sight o' the mountings, an' have
everything on a level."

" You said there was worse to tell behind," suggested Lyddy Bangs, as if it were
only common politeness to show an appre-
ciation of the friendly offering.

" I have it in mind to get round to that in
proper course," responded Mrs. Powder, a
trifle offended by the mild pertinacity. " I
settled it in my mind that I was goin' to tell
you somethin' for a kind of a treat the day
we come out blueberryin'. *There!*" — and
Mrs. Powder rose with difficulty from her
knees, and retreated pompously to the shade
of a hemlock-tree which grew over a shelv-
ing rock near by.

Lyddy Bangs could not resist picking a
little longer in an unusually fruitful spot;
then she hastened to seat herself by her
friend. It was no common occasion.

Mrs. Powder was very warm ; and further
evaded and postponed telling the secret by
wishing that she were as light on foot as her
companion, and deploring her increasing
weight.   Then she demanded a second sight
of the blueberries, which were compared and
decided upon as to quality and quantity.
Then the cat, which had been left at some
distance on her rock, came trotting toward
her mistress in a disturbed way, and after
a minute of security in a comfortable lap
darted away again in a strange, excited manner.

"She 's goin' to have a fit, I do believe!"
exclaimed Lyddy Bangs, quite disheartened,
for the cat was Mrs. Powder's darling and
she might leave everything to go in search
of her.

"She may have seen a snake or something. She often gets scared and runs home
when we 're out a-trarvelin'," said the cat's
owner, complacently, and Lyddy's spirits
rose again.

"I suppose you never suspected that
Ezra Barnet and Ruth Crosby cared the
least thing about one another?" inquired
the keeper of the secret a moment later, and
the listener turned toward Mrs. Powder
with a startled face.

"Now, Harri't Powder, for mercy's sakes alive!" was all that she could say; but Mrs. Powder was satisfied, and confirmed the amazing news by a most emphatic nod.

"My lawful sakes! what be they goin' to do about it?" inquired Lyddy Bangs, flushing with excitement. "A Barnet an' a Crosby fall in love! Don't you rec'lect how the old ones was al'ays fightin' and callin' names when we was all to school together? Times is changed, certain."

"Now, say you hope to die if ever you'll tell a word I say," pursued Mrs. Powder. "If I was to be taken away to-morrow, you'd be all the one that would know it except Mis' Crosby and Ezra and Ruth themselves. 'T was nothin' but her bein' nigh to death that urged her to tell me the state o' things. I s'pose she thought I might favor 'em in time to come. Abby Crosby she says to me, 'Mis' Powder, my poor girl may need your motherin' care.' An' I says, 'Mis' Crosby, she shall have it;' and then she had a spasm o' pain, and we harped no more that day as I remember."

"How come it about? I shouldn't have told anybody that asked me that a Barnet and a Crosby ever 'changed the time o' day,

much less kep' company," protested the listener.

"Kep' company! pore young creatur's!"
said Mrs. Powder. "They 've hid 'em away
in the swamps an' hollers, and in the edge o'
the growth, at nightfall, for the sake o' gittin' a word; an' they 've stole out, shiverin',
into that plaguy lane o' winter nights. I
tell ye I 've heard hifalutin' folks say that
love would still be lord of all, but I never
was 'strained to believe it till I see what that
boy and girl was willin' to undergo. All
the hate of all their folks is turned to love
in them, and I couldn't help a-watchin' of
'em. An' I ventured to send Ruth over to
my house after my alpaccy aprin, and then
I made an arrant out to the spring-brook to
see if there was any cresses started — which
I knew well enough there wasn't — and I
spoke right out bold to Ezra, that was at
work on a piece of ditching over on his land.
'Ezra,' says I, 'if you git time, just run
over to the edge o' my pasture and pick me
a handful o' balm o' Gilead buds. I want
to put 'em in half a pint o' new rum for
Mis' Crosby, and there ain't a soul to send.'
I knew he 'd just meet her coming back, if
I could time it right gittin' of Ruth started.

He looked at me kind of curi's, and pretty quick I see him leggin' it over the fields with an axe and a couple o' ends o' board, like he'd got to mend a fence. I had to keep her dinner warm for her till ha'-past one o'clock. I don't know what he mentioned to his folks, but Ruth she come an' kissed me hearty when she first come inside the door. 'T is harder for Ezra; he ain't got nobody to speak to, and Ruth's got her mother if she is a Mis' Much-afraid."

"I don't know's we can blame Crosby for not wantin' to give his girl to the Barnets, after they've got away all his substance, his means, an' his cattle, like 't was in the Book o' Job," urged Lyddy Bangs. "Seems as if they might call it square an' marry the young folks off, but they won't nohow; 't will only fan the flame." Lyddy Bangs was a sentimental person; neighbor Powder had chosen wisely in gaining a new friend to the cause of Ezra Barnet's apparently hopeless affection. Unknown to herself, however, she had been putting the lover's secret to great risk of untimely betrayal.

The weather was most beautiful that afternoon; there was an almost intoxicating freshness and delight among the sweet odors of the hillside pasture, and the two elderly women were serene at heart and felt like girls again as they talked together. They remembered many an afternoon like this; they grew more and more confiding as they reviewed the past and their life-long friendship. A stranger might have gathered only the most rural and prosaic statements, and a tedious succession of questions, from what Mrs. Powder and Lyddy Bangs had to say to each other, but the old stories of true love and faithful companionship were again simply rehearsed. Those who are only excited by more complicated histories too often forget that there are no new plots to the comedies and tragedies of life. They are played sometimes by country people in homespun, sometimes by townsfolk in velvet and lace. Love and prosperity, death and loss and misfortune — the stories weave themselves over and over again, never mind whether the ploughman or the wit of the clubs plays the part of hero.

The two homely figures sat still so long that they seemed to become permanent points in the landscape, and the small birds, and even a wary chipmunk, went their ways

unmindful of Mrs. Powder and Lyddy
Bangs. The old hemlock-tree, under which
they sat discoursing, towered high above the
young pine-growth which clustered thick behind them on the hillside. In the middle
of a comfortable reflection upon the Barnet
grandfather's foolishness or craftiness, Mrs.
Powder gave sudden utterance to the belief
that some creature up in the tree was dropping pieces of bark and cones all over her.

"A squirrel, most like," said Lyddy
Bangs, looking up into the dense branches.
"The tree is a-scatterin' down, ain't it? As
you was sayin', Grandsir Barnet must have
knowed well enough what he was about" —

"Oh, gorry! oh, git out! ow — o — w!"
suddenly wailed a voice overhead, and a desperate scramble and rustling startled the
good women half out of their wits. "Ow,
Mis' Powder!" shrieked a familiar voice,
while both hearts thumped fast, and Joel
came, half falling, half climbing, down out
of the tree. He bawled, and beat his head
with his hands, and at last rolled in agony
among the bayberry and lamb-kill. "Look
out for 'em!" he shouted. "Oh, gorry! I
thought 't was only an old last-year's hornet's
nest — they 'll sting you, too!"

Mrs. Powder untied her apron and laid about her with sure aim. Only two hornets were to be seen; but after these were beaten to the earth, and she stopped to regain her breath, Joel hardly dared to lift his head or to look about him.

"What was you up there for, anyhow?" asked Lyddy Bangs, with severe suspicion. "Harking to us, I'll be bound!" But Mrs. Powder, who knew Joel's disposition best, elbowed her friend into silence and began to inquire about the condition of his wounds. There was a deep-seated hatred between Joel and Miss Bangs.

"Oh, dear! they've bit me all over," groaned the boy. "Ain't you got somethin' you can rub on, Mis' Powder?"— and the rural remedy of fresh earth was suggested.

"'T is too dry here," said the adviser. "Just you step down to that ma'shy spot there by the brook, dear, and daub you with the wet mud real good, and 't will ease you right away." Mrs. Powder's voice sounded compassionate, but her spirit and temper of mind gave promise of future retribution.

"I'll teach him to follow us out eavesdropping, this fashion!" said Lyddy Bangs, when the boy had departed, weeping. "I'm more 'n gratified that the hornets got hold of him! I hope 't will serve him for a lesson."

" Don't you r'ile him up one mite, now," pleaded Mrs. Powder, while her eyes bore witness of hardly controlled anger. " He's the worst tattle-tale I ever see, and we've put ourselves into a trap. If he tells his mother she 'll spread it all over town. But I should no more thought o' his bein' up in that tree than o' his bein' the sarpent in the garden o' Eden. You leave Joel to me, and be mild with him 's you can."

The culprit approached, still lamenting. His ear and cheek were hugely swollen already, so that one eye was nearly closed. The blueberry expedition was relinquished, and with heavy sighs of dissatisfaction Lyddy Bangs took up the two half-filled pails, while Mrs. Powder kindly seized Joel by his small, thin hand, and the little group moved homeward across the pasture.

" Where's your hat?" asked Lyddy, stopping short, after they had walked a little distance.

" Hanging on a limb up by the wop's nest," answered Joel. " Oh, git me home, Mis' Powder!"

III.

No one would suspect, from the look of the lane itself, that it had always been such a provoker of wrath, and even a famous battle-ground. While petty wars had raged between the men and women of the old farms, walnut-trees had grown high in air, and apple-trees had leaned their heavy branches on the stone walls and, year after year, decked themselves in pink-and-white blossoms to arch this unlucky by-way for a triumphal procession of peace that never came. Birds built their nests in the boughs and pecked the ripe blackberries; green brakes and wild roses and tall barberry-bushes flourished in their season on either side the wheel-ruts. It was a remarkably pleasant country lane, where children might play and lovers might linger. No one would imagine that this lane had its lawsuits and damages, its annual crop of briefs, and succession of surveyors and quarrelsome partisans; or that in every generation of owners each man must be either plaintiff or defendant.

The surroundings looked permanent enough. No one would suspect that a cer-

tain piece of wall had been more than once
thrown down by night and built again, angrily, by day; or that a well-timbered corn-
house had been the cause of much litigation,
and even now looked, when you came to
know its story, as if it stood on its long,
straight legs, like an ungainly, top-heavy
beast, all ready to stalk away when its position became too dangerous. The Barnets
had built it beyond their boundary; it had
been moved two or three times, backward
and forward.

The Barnet house and land stood between
the Crosby farm and the high-road; the
Crosbys had never been able to reach the
highway without passing their enemies under
full fire of ugly looks or taunting voices.
The intricacies of legal complications in the
matter of right of way would be impossible
to explain. They had never been very clear
to any impartial investigator. Barnets and
Crosbys had gone to their graves with bitter
hatred and sullen desire for revenge in their
hearts. Perhaps this one great interest, outside the simple matters of food and clothing
and farmers' work, had taken the place to
them of drama and literature and art. One
could not help thinking, as he looked at the

decrepit fences and mossy, warped roofs and buckling walls, to how much better use so much money might have been put. The costs of court and the lawyers' fees had taken everything, and men had drudged, in heat and frost, and women had pinched and slaved to pay the lane's bills. Both the Barnet and Crosby of the present time stood well enough in the opinion of other neighbors. They were hard-fisted, honest men; the fight was inherited to begin with, and they were stubborn enough to hold fast to the fight. Law Lane was as well known as the county roads in half a dozen towns. Perhaps its irreconcilable owners felt a thrill of enmity that had come straight down from Scottish border-frays, as they glanced along its crooked length. Who could believe that the son and daughter of the warring households, instead of being ready to lift the torch in their turn, had weakly and misguidedly fallen in love with each other?

Nobody liked Mrs. Barnet. She was a cross-grained, suspicious soul, who was a tyrant and terror of discomfort in her own household whenever the course of events ran counter to her preference. Her son Ezra was a complete contrast to her in disposition,

and to his narrow-minded, prejudiced father
as well. The elder Ezra was capable of
better things, however, and might have been
reared to friendliness and justice, if the
Crosby of his youthful day had not been
specially aggravating and the annals of Law
Lane at their darkest page. If there had
been another boy to match young Ezra, on
the Crosby farm, the two might easily have
fostered their natural boyish rivalries until
something worse came into being; but when
one's enemy is only a sweet-faced little girl,
it is very hard to impute to her all manner
of discredit and serpent-like power of evil.
At least, so Ezra Barnet the younger felt in
his inmost heart; and though he minded his
mother for the sake of peace, and played his
solitary games and built his unapplauded
dams and woodchuck - traps on his own
side of the fences, he always saw Ruth
Crosby as she came and went, and liked her
better and better as years went by. When
the tide of love rose higher than the young
people's steady heads, they soon laid fast
hold of freedom. With all their perplexi-
ties, life was by no means at its worst, and
rural diplomacy must bend all its energies
to hinder these unexpected lovers.

Ezra Barnet had never so much as entered the Crosby house; the families were
severed beyond the reuniting power of even
a funeral. Ezra could only try to imagine
the room to which his Ruth had returned
one summer evening after he had left her,
reluctantly, because the time drew near for
his father's return from the village. His
mother had been in a peculiarly bad temper
all day, and he had been glad to escape
from her unwelcome insistence that he should
marry any one of two or three capable girls,
and so furnish some help in the housekeeping. Ezra had often heard this suggestion
of his duty, and, tired and provoked at last,
he had stolen out to the garden and wandered beyond it to the brook and out to the
fields. Somewhere, somehow, he had met
Ruth, and the lovers bewailed their trials
with unusual sorrow and impatience. It
seemed very hard to wait. Young Barnet
was ready to persuade the tearful girl that
they must go away together and establish a
peaceful home of their own. He was heartily
ashamed because the last verdict was in his
father's favor, and Ruth forebore to wound
him with any glimpse of the straits to which
her own father had been reduced. She was

too dutiful to leave the pinched household, where her help was needed more than ever; she persuaded her lover that they were sure to be happy at last — indeed, were not they happy now? How much worse it would be if they could not safely seize so many opportunities, brief though they were, of being together! If the fight had been less absorbing and the animosity less bitter, they might have been suspected long ago.

So Ruth and Ezra parted, with uncounted kisses, and Ezra went back to the dingy-walled kitchen, where his mother sat alone. It was hardly past twilight out of doors, but Mrs. Barnet had lighted a kerosene-lamp, and sat near the small open window mending a hot-looking old coat. She looked so needlessly uncomfortable and surly that her son was filled with pity, as he stood watching her, there among the moths and beetles that buffeted the lamp-chimney.

" Why don't you put down your sewing and come out a little ways up the road, mother, and get cooled off?" he asked, pleasantly; but she only twitched herself in her chair and snapped off another needleful of linen thread.

" I can't spare no time to go gallivantin',

like some folks," she answered. " I always
have had to work, and I always shall. I
see that Crosby girl mincin' by an hour ago,
as if she 'd be'n off all the afternoon. Folks
that think she 's so amiable about saving
her mother's strength would be surprised at
the way she dawdles round, I guess " — and
Mrs. Barnet crushed an offending beetle
with her brass thimble in a fashion that dis-
gusted Ezra. Somehow, his mother had a
vague instinct that he did not like to hear
sharp words about Ruth Crosby. Yet he
rarely had been betrayed into an ill-judged
defense. He had left Ruth only a minute
ago ; he knew exactly what she had been
doing all day, and from what kind errand
she had been returning ; the blood rushed
quickly to his face, and he rose from his seat
by the table and went out to the kitchen
doorstep. The air was cool and sweet, and
a sleepy bird chirped once or twice from an
elm-bough overhead. The moon was near
its rising, and he could see the great shapes
of the mountains that lay to the eastward.
He forgot his mother, and began to think
about Ruth again ; he wondered if she were
not thinking of him, and meant to ask her
if she remembered an especial feeling of

nearness just at this hour. Ezra turned to look at the clocks to mark the exact time.

" Yes," said Mrs. Barnet, as she saw him try to discover the hour, " 't is time that father was to home. I s'pose, bein' mail-night, everybody was out to the post-office to hear the news, and most like he 's bawlin' himself hoarse about fall 'lections or something. He ain't got done braggin' about our gittin' the case, neither. There 's always some new one that wants to git the p'ints right from headquarters. I did n't see Crosby go by, did you? "

" He 'd have had to foot it by the path 'cross-lots," replied Ezra, gravely, from the doorstep. " He 's sold his hoss."

" He ain't ! " exclaimed Mrs. Barnet, with a chuckle. " I s'pose they 're proddin' him for the money up to court. Guess he won't try to fight us again for one while."

Ezra said nothing; he could not bear this sort of thing much longer. " I won't be kept like a toad under a harrow," he muttered to himself. " I think it seems kind of hard," he ventured to say aloud. " Now he 's got to hire when fall work comes on, and " —

The hard-hearted woman within had long

been trying to provoke her peaceable son into an argument, and now the occasion had come. Ezra restrained himself from speech with a desperate effort, and stopped his ears to the sound of his mother's accusing voice. In the middle of her harangue a wagon was driven into the yard, and his father left it quickly and came toward the door.

"Come in here, you lout!" he shouted, angrily. "I want to look at you! I want to see what such a mean-spirited sneak has got to say for himself." Then changing his voice to a whine, he begged Ezra, who had caught him from falling as he stumbled over the step, "Come in, boy, an' tell me 't ain't true. I guess they was only thornin' of me up; you ain't took a shine to that Crosby . miss, now, have you?"

"No son of mine — no son of mine!" burst out the mother, who had been startled by the sudden entrance of the news-bringer. Her volubility was promptly set free, and Ezra looked from his father's face to his mother's.

"Father," said he, turning away from the scold, who was nearly inarticulate in her excess of rage — "father, I'd rather talk to you, if you want to hear what I've got to say. Mother's got no reason in her."

"Ezry," said the elder man, " I see how 't is. Let your ma'am talk all she will. I 'm broke with shame of ye ! " — his voice choked weakly in his throat. " Either you tell me 't is all nonsense, or you go out o' that door and shut it after you for good. An' ye 're all the boy I 've got."

The woman had stopped at last, mastered by the terror of the moment. Her husband's face was gray with passion ; her son's cheeks were flushed and his eyes were full of tears. Mrs. Barnet's tongue for once had lost its cunning.

The two men looked at each other as long as they could ; the younger man's eyes fell first. " I wish you would n't be hasty," he said ; " to-morrow " —

" You 've heard," was the only answer ; and in a moment more Ezra Barnet reached to the table and took his old straw hat which lay there.

" Good-by, father ! " he said, steadily. " I think you 're wrong, sir ; but I never meant to carry on that old fight and live like the heathen." And then, young and strong and angry, he left the kitchen.

" He might have took some notice o' me, if he 's goin' for good," said the mother spitefully; but her son did not hear this taunt, and the father only tottered where he stood. The moths struck against his face as if it were a piece of wood; he sank feebly into a chair, muttering, and trying to fortify himself in his spent anger.

Ezra went out, dazed and giddy. But he found the young horse wandering about the yard, eager for his supper and fretful at the strange delay. He unharnessed the creature and backed the wagon under the shed; then he turned and looked at the house — should he go in? No! The fighting instinct, which had kept firm grasp on father and grandfather, took possession of Ezra now. He crossed the yard and went out at the gate, and down the lane's end to the main road. The father and mother listened to his footsteps, and the man gave a heavy groan.

"Let him go — let him go! 't will teach him a lesson!" said Mrs. Barnet, with something of her usual spirit. She could not say more, though she tried her best; the occasion was far too great.

How many times that summer Mrs. Powder attempted to wreak vengeance upon Joel, the tattle-tale; into what depths of in-

termittent remorse the mischief-making boy
was resolutely plunged, who shall describe?
No more luncheons of generous provision;
no more jovial skirmishing at the kitchen
windows, or liberal payment for easy errands. Whenever Mrs. Powder saw Lyddy
Bangs, or any other intimate and sympathetic friend, she bewailed her careless confidences under the hemlock-tree and detailed
her anxious attentions to the hornet-stung
eavesdropper.

"I went right home," she would say, sorrowfully; "I filled him plumb-full with as
good a supper as I could gather up, and I
took all the fire out o' them hornit-stings
with the best o' remedies. 'Joel, dear,'
says I, 'you won't lose by it if you keep
your mouth shut about them words I spoke
to Lyddy Bangs,' and he was that pious I
might ha' known he meant mischief. They
ain't boys nor men, they're divils, when
they come to that size, and so you mark my
words! But his mother never could keep
nothing to herself, and I knew it from past
sorrers; and I never slept a wink that night
— sure 's you live — till the roosters crowed
for day."

"Perhaps 't won't do nothin' but good!"

Lyddy Bangs would say, consolingly. " Perhaps the young folks 'll git each other a sight the sooner. They 'd had to kep' it to theirselves till they was gray-headed, 'less somebody let the cat out o' the bag."

" Don't you rec'lect how my cat acted that day ! " exclaimed Mrs. Powder, excitedly. " How she was good as took with a fit ! She knowed well enough what was brewin' ; I only wish we 'd had half of her sense."

IV.

The day before Christmas all the long valley was white with deep, new-fallen snow. The road which led up from the neighboring village and the railroad station stretched along the western slope — a mere trail, untrodden and unbroken. The storm had just ceased ; the high mountain-peaks were clear and keen and rose-tinted with the waning light ; the hills were no longer green with their covering of pines and maples and beeches, but gray with bare branches, and a cold, dense color, almost black, where the evergreens grew thickest. On the other side of the valley the farmsteads were

mapped out as if in etching or pen-drawing;
the far-away orchards were drawn with a curious exactness and regularity, the crooked
boughs of the apple-trees and the longer
lines of the walnuts and ashes and elms came
out against the snow with clear beauty.
The fences and walls were buried in snow;
the farm-houses and barns were petty shapes
in their right-angled unlikeness to natural
growths. You were half amused, half
shocked, as the thought came to you of in-
different creatures called men and women,
who busied themselves within those narrow
walls, under so vast a sky, and fancied the
whole importance of the universe was belit-
tled by that of their few pent acres. What
a limitless world lay outside those play-
thing-farms, yet what beginnings of immor-
tal things the small gray houses had known!

The day before Christmas!— a festival
which seemed in that neighborhood to be of
modern origin. The observance of it was
hardly popular yet among the elder people,
but Christmas had been appropriated, never-
theless, as if everybody had felt the lack of
it. New Year's Day never was sufficient
for New England, even in its least mirthful

decades. For those persons who took true joy in life, something deeper was needed than the spread-eagle self-congratulations of the Fourth of July, or the family reunions of Thanksgiving Day. There were no bells ringing which the country-folks in Law Lane might listen for on Christmas Eve; but something more than the joy that is felt in the poorest dwelling when a little child, with all its possibilities, is born; something happier still came through that snowy valley with the thought of a Christmas-Child who "was the bringer-in and founder of the reign of the higher life." This was the greater Thanksgiving Day, when the whole of Christendom is called to praise and pray and hear the good-tidings, and every heart catches something of the joyful inspirations of good-will to men.

Ezra Barnet sat on a fallen tree from which he had brushed the powdery snow. It was hard work wading through the drifts, and he had made good headway up the long hill before he stopped to rest. Across the valley in the fading daylight he saw the two farms, and could even trace the course of Law Lane itself, marked by the well-known trees.

How small his own great nut-tree looked at this distance! The two houses, with their larger and smaller out-buildings and snow-topped woodpiles, looked as if they had crept near together for protection and companionship. There were no other houses within a wide space. Ezra knew how remote the homes really were from each other, judged by any existing sympathy and interest. He thought of his bare, unnourished boyhood with something like resentment; then he remembered how small had been his parents' experience, what poor ambition had been fostered in them by their lives; even his mother's impatience with the efforts he had made to bring a little more comfort and pleasantness to the old farm-house was thought of with pity for her innate lack of pleasure in pleasant things. Ezra himself was made up of inadequacies, being born and bred of the Barnets. He was at work on the railroad now, with small pay; but he had always known that there could be something better than the life in their farm-house, while his mother did not. A different feeling came over him as he thought whom the other farm-house sheltered; he had looked for that first, to see if it were stand-

ing safe. Ruth's last letter had come only
the day before. This Christmas holiday
was to be a surprise to her. He wondered
whether Ruth's father would let him in.

Never mind! he could sleep in the barn
among the hay; and Ezra dropped into the
snow again from the old tree-trunk and went
his way. There was a small house just past
a bend in the road, and he quickened his
steps toward it. Alas! there was no smoke
in Mrs. Powder's chimney. She was away
on one of her visiting tours; nursing some
sick person, perhaps. She would have
housed him for the night most gladly; now
he must take his chances in Law Lane.

The darkness was already beginning to
fall; there was a curious brownness in the
air, like summer twilight; the cold air became
sharper, and the young man shivered a little
as he walked. He could not follow the left-
hand road, where it led among hospitable
neighbors, but turned bravely off toward his
old home — a long, lonely walk at any time
of the year, among woods and thickets all
well known to him, and as familiar as they
were to the wild creatures that haunted
them. Yet Ezra Barnet did not find it easy
to whistle as he went along.

Suddenly, from behind a scrub-oak that was heavily laden with dead leaves and snow, leaped a small figure, and Ezra was for the moment much startled. The boy carried a rabbit-trap with unusual care, and placed it on the snow-drift before which he stood waist-deep already. "Gorry, Ezry! you most scared me to pieces!" said Joel, in a perfectly calm tone. "Wish you Merry Christmas! Folks 'll be lookin' for you; they did n't s'pose you 'd git home before to-morrow, though."

"Looking for me?" repeated the young man, with surprise. "I did n't send no word " —

"Ain't you heard nothin' 'bout your ma'am's being took up for dead?"

"No, I ain't; and you ain't foolin' me with your stories, Joel Smith? You need n't play off any of your mischief onto me."

"What you gittin' mad with me about?" inquired Joel, with a plaintive tone in his voice. "She got a fall out in the barn this mornin', an' it liked to killed her. Most folks ain't heard nothin' 'bout it 'cause its been snowin' so. They come for Mis' Powder and she called out to our folks, as they brought her round by the way of Asa Pack-

er's store to git some opodildack or somethin'.''

Ezra asked no more questions, but strode
past the boy, who looked after him a moment, and then lifted the heavy box-trap and
started homeward. The imprisoned rabbit
had been snowed up since the day before at
least, and Joel felt humane anxieties, else he
would have followed Ezra at a proper distance and learned something of his reception.

Mrs. Powder was reigning triumphant in
the Barnet house, being nurse, housekeeper,
and spiritual adviser all in one. She had
been longing for an excuse to spend at least
half a day under that cheerless roof for
many months, but occasion had not offered.
She found the responsibility of the parted
lovers weighing more and more heavily on
her mind, and had set her strong will at
work to find some way of reuniting them,
and even to restore a long-banished peace to
the farms. She would not like to confess
that a mild satisfaction caused her heart to
feel warm and buoyant when an urgent sum-
mons had come at last; but such was the
simple truth. A man who had been felling

trees on the farm brought the news, melancholy to hear under other circumstances, that Mrs. Barnet had been hunting eggs in a stray nest in the hay-mow, and had slipped to the floor and been taken up insensible. Bones were undoubtedly broken; she was a heavy woman, and had hardly recovered her senses. The doctor must be found as soon as possible. Mrs. Powder hastily put her house to rights, and, with a good round bundle of what she called her needments, set forth on the welcome enterprise. On the way she could hardly keep herself from undue cheerfulness, and if ever there was likely to be a reassuring presence in a sick-room it was Harriet Powder's that December day.

She entered the gloomy kitchen looking like a two-footed snow-drift, her big round shoulders were so heaped with the damp white flakes. Old Ezra Barnet sat by the stove in utter despair, and waved a limp hand warningly toward the bedroom door.

"She's layin' in a sog," he said, hopelessly. "I ought to thought to send word to pore Ezry — all the boy she ever had."

Mrs. Powder calmly removed her snowy outer garments, and tried to warm her hands over the fire.

" Put in a couple o' sticks of good dry wood," she suggested, in a soothing voice; and the farmer felt his spirits brighten, he knew not why. Then the whole - souled, hearty woman walked into the bedroom.

" All I could see," she related afterward, " was the end of Jane Barnet's nose, and I was just as sure then as I be now that she was likely to continner; but I set down side of the bed and got holt of her hand, and she groaned two or three times real desperate. I wished the doctor was there, to see if anything really ailed her; but I someways knowed there wa'n't, 'less 't was gittin' over such a jounce. I spoke to her, but she never said nothin', and I went back out into the kitchen. 'She's a very sick woman,' says I, loud enough for her to hear me; I knew 't would please her. There was a good deal to do, and I put on my aprin and took right holt and begun to lay about me and git dinner; the men-folks was wiltin' for want o' somethin', it being nigh three o'clock. An' then I got Jane to feel more comfortable with ondressin' of her, for all she 'd hardly let me touch of her — poor creatur', I expect she did feel sore! — and then daylight was failin' and I felt kind o' spent, so

I set me down in a cheer by the bed-head and was speechless, too. I knew if she was able to speak she could n't hold in no great spell longer.

"After a while she stirred a little and groaned, and then says she, 'Ain't the doctor comin'?' And I peaced her up well 's I could. 'Be I very bad off, Harri't?' says she.

"'We 'll hope for the best, Jane,' says I; and that minute the notion come to me how I 'd work her round, an' I like to laughed right out, but I did n't.

"'If I should lose me again, you must see to sendin' for my son,' says she; 'his father 's got no head.'

"'I will,' says I, real solemn. 'An' you can trust me with anything you feel to say, sister Barnet.'

"She kind of opened her eye that was next to me and surveyed my countenance sharp, but I looked serious, and she groaned real honest. 'Be I like old Mis' Topliff?' she whispered, and I kind o' nodded an' put my hand up to my eyes. She *was* like her, too; some like her, but not nigh so bad, for Mis' Topliff was hurt so fallin' down the sullar-stairs that she never got over it an' died the day after.

" ' Oh, my sakes ! ' she bu'st out whinin',
' I can't be took away now. I ain't a-goin'
to die right off, be I, Mis' Powder ? '

" ' I ain't the one to give ye hope. In the
midst of life we are in death. We ain't
sure of the next minute, none of us,' says I,
meanin' it general, but discoursin' away like
an old book o' sermons.

" ' I do feel kind o' failin', now,' says she.
' Oh, can't you do nothin'?' — and I come
over an' set on the foot o' the bed an' looked
right at her. I knew she was a dreadful
notional woman, and always made a fuss
when anything was the matter with her;
could n't bear no kind o' pain.

" ' Sister Barnet,' says I, ' don't you bear
nothin' on your mind you 'd like to see
righted before you go? I know you ain't
been at peace with Crosby's folks, and
't ain't none o' my business, but I should n't
want to be called away with hard feelin's in
my heart. You must overlook my speaking
right out, but I should want to be so used
myself.'

" Poor old creatur' ! She had an awful
fight of it, but she beat her temper for once
an' give in. ' I do forgive all them Crosbys,' says she, an' rolled up her eyes. I

says to myself that wa'n't all I wanted, but I let her alone a spell, and set there watchin' as if I expected her to breathe her last any minute.

"She asked for Barnet, and I said he was anxious and out watchin' for the doctor, now the snow'd stopped. 'I wish I could see Ezra,' says she. 'I 'm all done with the lane now, and I 'd keep the peace if I was goin' to live.' Her voice got weak, and I did n't know but she was worse off than I s'posed. I was scared for a minute, and then I took a grain o' hope. I 'd watched by too many dyin'-beds not to know the difference.

"'Don't ye let Barnet git old Nevins to make my coffin, will ye, Mis' Powder?' says she once.

"'He 's called a good workman, ain't he?' says I, soothin' as I could. When it come to her givin' funeral orders, 't was more 'n I could do to hold in.

"'I ain't goin' snappin' through torment in a hemlock coffin, to please that old cheat!' says she, same 's if she was well, an' ris' right up in bed; and then her bruises pained her an' she dropped back on the pillow.

" ' Oh, I 'm a-goin' now ! ' says she.
' I 've been an awful hard woman. 'T was
I put Barnet up to the worst on 't. I 'm
willin' Ezra should marry Ruthy Crosby ;
she 's a nice, pooty gal, and I never owned
it till now I 'm on my dyin'-bed — Oh, I 'm
a-goin', I 'm a-goin' ! — Ezra can marry her,
and the two farms together 'll make the best
farm in town. Barnet ain't got no fight
left ; he 's like an old sheep since we drove
off Ezra.' And then she 'd screech ; you
never saw no such a fit of narves. And the
end was I had to send to Crosby's, in all the
snow, for them to come over.

" An' Barnet was got in to hold her hand
and hear last words enough to make a
Fourth o' July speech ; and I was sent out
to the door to hurry up the Crosbys, and
who should come right out o' the dark but
Ezra. I declare, when I see him you could
a-knocked me down with a feather. But I
got him by the sleeve — ' You hide away a
spell,' says I, ' till I set the little lamp in
this winder ; an' don't you make the best o'
your ma's condition ; 'pear just as consarned
about her as you can. I 'll let ye know
why, soon 's we can talk ' — and I shoved
him right out an' shut the door.

" The groans was goin' on, and in come Crosby and Ruth, lookin' scared about to death themselves. Neither on 'em had ever been in that house before, as I know of. She called 'em into the bedroom and said she 'd had hard feelin's towards them and wanted to make peace before she died, and both on 'em shook hands with her.

" ' Don't you want to tell Ruth what you said to me about her and Ezry ? ' says I, whisperin' over the bed. ' 'Live or dead, you know 't is right and best.'

" ' There ain't no half way 'bout me,' she says, and so there wa'n't. ' Ruth,' says she, out loud, ' I want you to tell pore Ezra that I gave ye both my blessin',' and I made two steps acrost that kitchen and set the lamp in the window, and in comes Ezra — pore boy, he did n't know what was brewin', and thought his mother was dyin' certain when he saw the Crosbys goin' in.

" He went an' stood beside the bed, an' his father clutched right holt of him. Thinks I to myself, if you make as edifyin' an end when your time really does come, you may well be thankful, Jane Barnet !

" They was all a-weepin', an' I was weepin' myself, if you 'll believe it, I 'd got

a-goin' so. You ought to seen her take holt
o' Ruth's hand an' Ezra's an' put 'em together. *Then* I'd got all I wanted, I tell
you. An' after she'd screeched two or
three times more she begun to git tired; the
poor old creatur' was shook up dreadful,
and I felt for her consid'able, though you
may not think it; so I beckoned 'em out
into the kitchen an' went in an' set with her
alone. She dropped off into a good easy
sleep, an' I told the folks her symptoms was
more encouragin'.

"I tell you, if ever I took handsome care
o' any sick person 't was Jane Barnet, before
she got about again; an' Ruth she used to
come over an' help real willin'. She got
holt of her ma'-in-law's bunnit one afternoon an' trimmed it up real tasty, and that
pleased Mis' Barnet about to death. My
conscience pricked me some, but not a great
sight. I'm willin' to take what blame come
to me by rights.

"The doctor come postin' along, late that
night, and said she was doin' well, owin' to
the care she'd had, and give me a wink.
And she's alive yet," Mrs. Powder always
assured her friends, triumphantly — "and,
what's more, is middlin' peaceable disposed.

She 's said one or two p'inted things to me,
though, an' I should n't wonder, come to
think it over, if she mistrusted me just the
least grain. But, dear sakes! they never
was so comfortable in their lives; an' Ezra
he got a first-rate bargain for a lot o' Crosby's woodland that the railroad wanted, and
peace is kind o' set in amon'st 'em up in
Law Lane."

V.

When Ezra Barnet waked on Christmas
morning, in his familiar, dark little chamber under the lean-to roof, he could hardly
believe that he was at home again, and that
such strange things had happened. There
were cheerful voices in the kitchen below,
and he dressed hurriedly and went downstairs.

There was Mrs. Powder, cooking the
breakfast with lavish generosity, and beaming with good-nature. Barnet, the father,
was smiling and looking on with pleased anticipation; the sick woman was comfortably
bolstered up in the bedroom. In all his life
the son had never felt so drawn to his
mother; there was a new look in her eyes as

he went toward her; she had lost her high color, and looked at him pleadingly, as she never had done before. "Ezry, come close here!" said she. "I believe I'm goin' to git about ag'in, after all. Mis' Powder says I be; but them feelin's I had slippin' down the mow, yesterday, was twice as bad as the thump I struck with. I may never be the same to work, but I ain't goin' to fight with folks no more, sence the Lord 'll let me live a spell longer. I ain't a-goin' to fight with nobody, no matter how bad I want to. Now, you go an' git you a good breakfast. I ain't eat a mouthful since breakfast yesterday, and you can bring me a help o' anything Sister Powder favors my havin'."

"I hope 't will last," muttered Sister Powder to herself, as she heaped the blue plate. "Wish you all a Merry Christmas!" she said. "I like to forgot my manners."

It was Christmas Day, whether anybody in Law Lane remembered it or not. The sun shone bright on the sparkling snow, the eaves were dropping, and the snow-birds and blue-jays came about the door. The wars of Law Lane were ended.

A LOST LOVER.

For a great many years it had been understood in Longfield that Miss Horatia Dane once had a lover, and that he been lost at sea. By little and little, in one way and another, her acquaintances found out or made up the whole story; and Miss Dane stood in the position, not of an unmarried woman exactly, but rather of having spent most of her life in a long and lonely widowhood. She looked like a person with a history, strangers often said (as if we each did not have a history); and her own unbroken reserve about this romance of hers gave everybody the more respect for it.

The Longfield people paid willing deference to Miss Dane: her family had always been one that could be liked and respected and she was the last that was left in the old home of which she was so fond. This was a high, square house, with a row of pointed windows in its roof, a peaked porch in front, with some lilac-bushes near it; and down by the road was a long, orderly procession of poplars, like a row of sentinels standing guard. She had lived here alone since her father's death, twenty years before. She was a kind, just woman whose pleasures were of a stately and sober sort; and she seemed not unhappy in her loneliness, though she sometimes said gravely that she was the last of her family, as if the fact had a great sadness for her.

She had some middle-aged and elderly cousins who lived at a distance, and they came occasionally to see her; but there had been no young people staying in her house for many years until this summer, when the daughter of her youngest cousin had written to ask if she might come to make a visit. She was a motherless girl of twenty, both older and younger than her years. Her father and brother, who were civil engineers, had taken some work upon the line of a railway in the far Western country. Nelly had made many long journeys with them before and since she had left school, and she had meant to follow them now, after spending a fortnight with the old cousin whom she had not seen since her childhood.

Her father had laughed at this visit as a freak, and warned her of the dullness and primness of Longfield; but the result was that the girl found herself very happy in the comfortable home. She was still her own free, unfettered, lucky, and sunshiny self; and the old house was so much pleasanter for the girlish face and life, that Miss Horatia had, at first timidly and then most heartily, begged her to stay for the whole summer, or even the autumn, until her father was ready to come East. The name of Dane was very dear to Miss Horatia, and she grew fonder of her guest. When the village people saw her glance at the girl affectionately, as they sat together in the family pew of a Sunday, or saw them walking together after tea, they said it was a good thing for Miss Horatia; how bright she looked! and no doubt she would leave all her money to Nelly Dane, if she played her cards well.

But we will do Nelly justice, and say that she was not mercenary; she would have scorned such a thought. She had grown to have a great love for her cousin Horatia, and really liked to please her. She idealized her, I have no doubt; and her repres-

sion, her grave courtesy and rare words of
approval, had a great fascination for a girl
who had just been used to people who chattered, and were upon most intimate terms
with you directly, and could forget you with
equal ease. And Nelly liked having so ad-
miring and easily pleased an audience as
Miss Dane and her old servant Melissa.
She liked to be queen of her company: she
had so many gay, bright stories of what had
happened to herself and her friends. Beside, she was clever with her needle, and
had all those practical gifts which elderly
women approve so heartily in girls. They
liked her pretty clothes; she was sensible,
and economical, and busy; they praised her
to each other and to the world, and even
stubborn old Andrew, the man servant to
whom Miss Horatia herself spoke with deference, would do anything she asked. Nelly
would by no means choose so dull a life as
this for the rest of her days; but she enjoyed it immensely for the time being. She
instinctively avoided all that would shock
the grave dignity and old-school ideas of
Miss Dane; and somehow she never had
felt happier or better satisfied with life.
Perhaps it was because she was her best and

most lady-like self. It was not long before
she knew the village people almost as well
as Miss Dane did, and she became a very
great favorite, as a girl so easily can who is
good-natured and pretty, and well versed in
city fashions; who has the tact and clever-
ness that come to such a nature from going
about the world and knowing many people.

She had not been in Longfield many
weeks before she heard something of Miss
Dane's love-story; for one of her new friends
asked, in a confidential moment, " Does your
cousin ever speak to you about the young
man to whom she was engaged to be married?" And Nelly answered, " No," with
great wonder, and not without regret at her
own ignorance. After this she kept eyes
and ears open for whatever news of this
lover's existence might be found.

At last it happened one morning that she
had a good chance for a friendly talk with
Melissa; for who should know the family
affairs better than she? Miss Horatia had
taken her second-best parasol, with a deep
fringe, and had gone majestically down the
street to do some household errands which
she could trust to no one. Melissa was
shelling peas at the shady kitchen doorstep,

and Nelly came strolling round from the garden, along the clean-swept flag-stones, and sat down to help her. Melissa moved along, with a grim smile, to make room for her. "You need n't bother yourself," said she. "I 've nothing else to do. You 'll green your fingers all over." But she was evidently pleased to have company.

" My fingers will wash," said Nelly, " and I 've nothing else to do either. Please push the basket this way a little, or I shall scatter the pods, and then you will scold." She went to work busily, while she tried to think of the best way to find out the story she wished to hear.

" There! " said Melissa, " I never told Miss H'ratia to get some citron, and I settled yesterday to make some pound-cake this forenoon after I got dinner along a piece. She 's most out o' mustard too; she 's set about having mustard to eat with her beef, just as the old colonel was before her. I never saw any other folks eat mustard with their roast beef; but every family has their own tricks. I tied a thread round my left-hand little finger purpose to remember that citron before she came down this morning. I hope I ain't losing my fac'lties." It was seldom that Melissa was so talkative as this at first. She was clearly in a talkative mood.

"Melissa," asked Nelly, with great bravery, after a minute or two of silence, "who was it that my cousin Horatia was going to marry? It's odd that I should n't know; but I don't remember father's ever speaking of it, and I should n't think of asking her."

"I s'pose it 'll seem strange to you," said Melissa, beginning to shell the peas a great deal faster, "but as many years as I have lived in this house with her, — her mother, the old lady, fetched me up, — I never knew Miss H'ratia to say a word about him. But there! she knows I know, and we 've got an understanding on many things we never talk over as some folks would. I 've heard about it from other folks. She was visiting her great-aunt in Salem when she met with him. His name was Carrick, and it was presumed they was going to be married when he came home from the voyage he was lost on. He had the promise of going out master of a new ship. They did n't keep company long; it was made up of a sudden, and folks here did n't get hold of the story till some time after. I 've heard some that ought to know say it was only talk, and they never was engaged to be married no more than I am."

"You say he was lost at sea?" asked Nelly.

"The ship never was heard from. They supposed she was run down in the night out in the South Seas somewhere. It was a good while before they gave up expecting news; but none ever come. I think she set everything by him, and took it very hard losing of him. But there! she'd never say a word. You're the freest-spoken Dane I ever saw; but you may take it from your mother's folks. I expect he gave her that whale's tooth with the ship drawn on it that's on the mantelpiece in her room. She may have a sight of other keepsakes, for all I know; but it ain't likely." And here there was a pause, in which Nelly grew sorrowful as she thought of the long waiting for tidings of the missing ship, and of her cousin's solitary life. It was very odd to think of prim Miss Horatia's being in love with a sailor. There was a young lieutenant in the navy whom Nelly herself liked dearly, and he had gone away on a long voyage. "Perhaps she's been just as well off," said Melissa. "She's dreadful set, y'r

cousin H'ratia is, and sailors is high-tem-
pered men. I've heard it hinted that he
was a fast fellow; and if a woman's got a
good home like this, and's able to do for
herself, she'd better stay there. I ain't
going to give up a certainty for an uncer-
tainty, — that's what *I* always tell 'em,"
added Melissa, with great decision, as if she
were besieged by lovers; but Nelly smiled
inwardly as she thought of the courage it
would take to support any one who wished
to offer her companion his heart and hand.
It would need desperate energy to scale the
walls of that garrison.

The green peas were all shelled presently,
and Melissa said gravely that she should
have to be lazy now until it was time to put
in the meat. She wasn't used to being
helped, unless there was extra work, and she
calculated to have one piece of work join on
to another. However, it was no account,
and she was obliged for the company; and
Nelly laughed merrily as she stood washing
her hands in the shining old copper basin at
the sink. The sun would not be round that
side of the house for a long time yet, and
the pink and blue morning-glories were still
in their full bloom and freshness. They

grew over the window, twined on strings exactly the same distance apart. There was a box crowded full of green houseleeks down at the side of the door; they were straying over the edge, and Melissa stooped stiffly down with an air of disapproval at their untidiness. "They straggle all over everything," said she, "and they're no kind of use, only Miss's mother, she set everything by 'em. She fetched 'em from home with her when she was married, her mother kep' a box, and they came from England. Folks used to say they was good for bee stings." Then she went into the inner kitchen, and Nelly went slowly away along the flag-stones to the garden from whence she had come. The garden-gate opened with a tired creak, and shut with a clack; and she noticed how smooth and shiny the wood was where the touch of so many hands had worn it. There was a great pleasure to this girl in finding herself among such old and well-worn things. She had been for a long time in cities, or at the West; and among the old fashions and ancient possessions of Longfield it seemed to her that everything had its story, and she liked the quietness and unchangeableness with which life seemed to go on from year to year. She had seen many a dainty or gorgeous garden, but never one that she had liked so well as this, with its herb-bed and its broken rows of currant-bushes, its tall stalks of white lilies, and its wandering rose-bushes and honeysuckles, that had bloomed beside the straight paths for so many more summers than she herself had lived. She picked a little bouquet of late red roses, and carried it into the house to put on the parlor table. The wide hall-door was standing open, with its green outer blinds closed, and the old hall was dim and cool. Miss Horatia did not like a glare of sunlight, and she abhorred flies with her whole heart. Nelly could hardly see her way through the rooms, it had been so bright out of doors; but she brought the tall champagne-glass of water from the dining-room and put the flowers in their place. Then she looked at two silhouettes which stood on the mantel in carved ebony frames. They were portraits of an uncle of Miss Dane and his wife. Miss Dane had thought Nelly looked like this uncle the evening before. She could not see the likeness herself; but the pictures suggested something else, and she turned suddenly, and went hurrying up the stairs

to Miss Horatia's own room, where she remembered to have seen a group of silhouettes fastened to the wall. There were
seven or eight, and she looked at the young
men among them most carefully; but they
were all marked with the name of Dane:
they were Miss Horatia's uncles and broth-
ers, and our friend hung them on their little
brass hooks again with a feeling of disappointment. Perhaps her cousin had a quaint
miniature of the lover, painted on ivory, and
shut in a worn red morocco case; she hoped
she should get a sight of it some day. This
story of the lost sailor had a wonderful
charm for the girl. Miss Horatia had never
been so interesting to her before. How she
must have mourned for the lover, and missed
him, and hoped there would yet be news
from the ship! Nelly thought she would
tell her own little love - story some day,
though there was not much to tell yet, in
spite of there being so much to think about.
She built a little castle in Spain as she sat
in the front window-seat of the upper hall,
and dreamed pleasant stories for herself
until the sharp noise of the front gate-latch
waked her; and she looked out through the
blind to see her cousin coming up the walk.

Miss Horatia looked hot and tired, and
her thoughts were not of any fashion of romance. "It is going to be very warm," said
she. "I have been worrying ever since I
have been gone, because I forgot to ask Andrew to pick those white currants for the
minister's wife. I promised that she should
have them early this morning. Would you
go out to the kitchen and ask Melissa to
step in for a moment, my dear?"

Melissa was picking over red currants to
make a pie, and rose from her chair with a
little unwillingness. "I guess they could
wait until afternoon," said she, as she came
back. "Miss H'ratia's in a fret because
she forgot about sending some white currants to the minister's. I told her that Andrew had gone to have the horses shod, and
wouldn't be back till near noon. I don't
see why part of the folks in the world should
kill themselves trying to suit the rest. As
long as I haven't got any citron for the
cake, I suppose I might go out and pick
'em," added Melissa ungraciously. "I'll
get some to set away for tea anyhow."

Miss Dane had a letter to write after she
had rested from her walk; and Nelly soon
left her in the dark parlor, and went back

to the sunshiny garden to help Melissa, who seemed to be taking life with more than her usual disapproval. She was sheltered by an enormous gingham sunbonnet.

"I set out to free my mind to your cousin H'ratia this morning," said she, as Nelly crouched down at the opposite side of the bush where she was picking; "but we can't agree on that p'int, and it's no use. I don't say nothing. You might's well ask the moon to face about and travel the other way as to try to change Miss H'ratia's mind. I ain't going to argue it with her, it ain't my place; I know that as well as anybody. She'd run her feet off for the minister's folks any day; and though I do say he's a fair preacher, they have n't got a speck o' consideration nor fac'lty; they think the world was made for them, but I think likely they'll find out it was n't; most folks do. When he first was settled here, I had a fit o' sickness, and he come to see me when I was getting over the worst of it. He did the best he could, I always took it very kind of him; but he made a prayer and he kep' sayin' 'this aged handmaid,' I should think a dozen times. Aged handmaid!" said Melissa scornfully; "I don't call myself aged yet, and that was more than ten years ago. I never made pretensions to being younger than I am; but you 'd 'a' thought I was a topplin' old creatur' going on a hundred."

Nelly laughed. Melissa looked cross, and moved on to the next currant-bush. "So that's why you don't like the minister?" But the question did not seem to please.

" I hope I never should be set against a preacher by such as that." And Nelly hastened to change the subject; but there was to be a last word: " I like to see a minister that's solid minister right straight through, not one of these veneered folks. But old Parson Croden spoilt me for setting under any other preaching."

" I wonder," said Nelly after a little, " if Cousin Horatia has any picture of that Captain Carrick."

" He was n't captain," said Melissa. " I never heard that it was any more than they talked of giving him a ship next voyage."

" And you never saw him? He never came here to see her?"

" Bless you, no! She met with him at Salem, where she was spending the winter, and he went right away to sea. I 've heard a good deal more about it of late years than

I ever did at the time. I suppose the Salem
folks talked about it enough. All I know
is, there was other good matches that offered
to her since, and could n't get her; and I
suppose it was on account of her heart's
being buried in the deep with *him*." And
this unexpected bit of sentiment, spoken in
Melissa's grum tone, seemed so funny to her
young companion, that she bent very low
to pick from a currant-twig close to the
ground, and could not ask any more questions for some time.

"I have seen her a sight o' times when I
knew she was thinking about him," Melissa
went on presently, this time with a tender-
ness in her voice that touched Nelly's heart.
"She's been dreadful lonesome. She and
the old colonel, her father, was n't much
company to each other, and she always kep'
everything to herself. The only time she
ever said a word to me was one night six or
seven years ago this Christmas. They got
up a Christmas-tree in the vestry, and she
went, and I did too; I guess everybody in
the whole church and parish that could crawl
turned out to go. The children they made
a dreadful racket. I'd ha' got my ears took
off if I had been so forth-putting when I

was little. I was looking round for Miss
H'ratia 'long at the last of the evening, and
somebody said they 'd seen her go home. I
hurried, and I could n't see any light in
the house, and I was afraid she was sick
or something. She come and let me in, and
I see she had been a-cryin'. I says, 'Have
you heard any bad news?' But she says,
' No,' and began to cry again, real pitiful.
' I never felt so lonesome in my life,' says
she, ' as I did down there. It 's a dreadful
thing to be left all alone in the world.' I
did feel for her; but I could n't seem to
say a word. I put some pine chips I had
handy for morning on the kitchen fire, and
I made her up a cup o' good hot tea quick 's
I could, and took it to her; and I guess
she felt better. She never went to bed till
three o'clock that night. I could n't shut my
eyes till I heard her come upstairs. There!
I set everything by Miss H'ratia. I have n't
got no folks either. I was left an orphan
over to Deerfield, where Miss's mother come
from, and she took me out o' the town-farm
to bring up. I remember when I come
here, I was so small I had a box to stand up
on when I helped wash the dishes. There 's
nothing I ain't had to make me comfortable,

and I do just as I 'm a mind to, and call in
extra help every day of the week if I give
the word ; but I 've had my lonesome times,
and I guess Miss II'ratia knew."

Nelly was very much touched by this bit
of a story, it was a new idea to her that Melissa should have so much affection and be
so sympathetic. People never will get over
being surprised that chestnut-burrs are not
as rough inside as they are outside, and the
girl's heart warmed toward the old woman
who had spoken with such unlooked-for sentiment and pathos. Melissa went to the
house with her basket, and Nelly also went
in, but only to put on another hat, and see
if it were straight in a minute spent before the old mirror, before she hurried down
the long elm-shaded street to buy a pound
of citron for the cake. She left it on the
kitchen table when she came back, and nobody ever said anything about it; only
there were two delicious pound-cakes — a
heart and a round — on a little blue china
plate beside Nelly's plate at tea.

After tea, Nelly and Miss Dane sat in
the front doorway, — the elder woman in a
high-backed chair, and the younger on the
door-step. The tree-toads and crickets were

tuning up heartily, the stars showed a little through the trees, and the elms looked heavy and black against the sky. The fragrance of the white lilies in the garden blew through the hall. Miss Horatia was tapping the ends of her fingers together. Probably she was not thinking of anything in particular. She had had a very peaceful day, with the exception of the currants; and they had, after all, gone to the parsonage some time before noon. Beside this, the minister had sent word that the delay made no distress; for his wife had unexpectedly gone to Downton to pass the day and night. Miss Horatia had received the business letter for which she had been looking for several days; so there was nothing to regret deeply for that day, and there seemed to be nothing for one to dread on the morrow.

"Cousin Horatia," asked Nelly, "are you sure you like having me here? Are you sure I don't trouble you?"

"Of course not," said Miss Dane, without a bit of sentiment in her tone; "I find it very pleasant having young company, though I am used to being alone; and I don't mind it as I suppose you would."

"I should mind it very much," said the girl softly.

"You would get used to it, as I have,"
said Miss Dane. "Yes, dear, I like having
you here better and better. I hate to think
of your going away." And she smoothed
Nelly's hair as if she thought she might have
spoken coldly at first, and wished to make
up for it. This rare caress was not without
its effect.

"I don't miss father and Dick so very
much," owned Nelly frankly, "because I
have grown used to their coming and going; but sometimes I miss people — Cousin
Horatia, did I ever say anything to you
about George Forest?"

"I think I remember the name," answered
Miss Dane.

"He is in the navy, and he has gone a
long voyage, and — I think everything of
him. I missed him awfully; but it is almost time to get a letter."

"Does your father approve of him?"
asked Miss Dane, with great propriety.
"You are very young yet, and you must not
think of such a thing carelessly. I should
be so much grieved if you threw away your
happiness."

"Oh! we are not really engaged," said
Nelly, who felt a little chilled. "I suppose

we are, too; only nobody knows yet. Yes, father knows him as well as I do, and he is very fond of him. Of course I should not keep it from father; but he guessed it himself. Only it's such a long cruise, Cousin Horatia, — three years, I suppose, — away off in China and Japan."

"I have known longer voyages than that," said Miss Dane, with a quiver in her voice; and she rose suddenly, and walked away, this grave, reserved woman, who seemed so contented and so comfortable. But when she came back, she asked Nelly a great deal about her lover, and learned more of the girl's life than she ever had before. And they talked together in the pleasantest way about this pleasant subject, which was so close to Nelly's heart, until Melissa brought the candles at ten o'clock, that being the hour of Miss Dane's bedtime.

But that night Miss Dane did not go to bed at ten; she sat by the window in her room, thinking. The moon rose late; and after a little while she blew out her candles, which were burning low. I suppose that the years which had come and gone since the young sailor went away on that last voyage of his had each added to her affection for him. She was a person who clung the more fondly to youth as she left it the farther behind.

This is such a natural thing; the great sorrows of our youth sometimes become the amusements of our later years; we can only remember them with a smile. We find that our lives look fairer to us, and we forget what used to trouble us so much, when we look back. Miss Dane certainly had come nearer to truly loving the sailor than she had any one else; and the more she thought of it, the more it became the romance of her life. She no longer asked herself, as she often had done in middle life, whether, if he had lived and had come home, she would have loved and married him. She had minded less and less, year by year, knowing that her friends and neighbors thought her faithful to the love of her youth. Poor, gay, handsome Joe Carrick! how fond he had been of her, and how he had looked at her that day he sailed away out of Salem Harbor on the brig Chevalier! If she had only known that she never should see him again, poor fellow!

But, as usual, her thoughts changed their current a little at the end of her reverie.

Perhaps, after all, loneliness was not so hard to bear as other sorrows. She had had a pleasant life, God had been very good to her, and had spared her many trials, and granted her many blessings. "I am an old woman now," she said to herself. "Things are better as they are; I can get on by myself better than most women can, and I never should have liked to be interfered with."

Then she shut out the moonlight, and lighted her candles again, with an almost guilty feeling. "What should I say if Nelly sat up till nearly midnight looking out at the moon?" she thought. "It is very silly; but this is such a beautiful night. I should like to have her see the moon shining through the tops of the trees." But Nelly was sleeping the sleep of the just and sensible in her own room.

Next morning at breakfast, Nelly was a little conscious of there having been uncommon confidences the night before; but Miss Dane was her usual calm and somewhat formal self, and proposed their making a few calls after dinner, if the weather were not too hot. Nelly at once wondered what she had better wear. There was a certain black

grenadine which Miss Horatia had noticed
with approval, and she remembered that the
lower ruffle needed hemming, and made up
her mind that she would devote most of
the time before dinner to that and to some
other repairs.　So, after breakfast was over,
she brought the dress downstairs, with her
work-box, and settled herself in the dining-
room.　Miss Dane usually sat there in the
morning; it was a pleasant room, and she
could keep an unsuspected watch over the
kitchen and Melissa, who did not need
watching in the least.　I dare say it was for
the sake of being within the sound of a
voice.

Miss Dane marched in and out that morning; she went upstairs, and came down
again, and was mysteriously busy for a while
in the parlor.　Nelly was sewing steadily by
a window, where one of the blinds was a little way open, and tethered in its place by a
string.　She hummed a tune to herself over
and over: —

" What will you do, love, when I am going,
　　With white sails flowing, the seas beyond ? "

And old Melissa, going to and fro at her
work in the kitchen, grumbled out bits of
an ancient psalm-tune at intervals.　There

seemed to be some connection between these fragments in her mind; it was like a ledge of rock in a pasture, that sometimes runs under the ground, and then crops out again. Perhaps it was the tune of Windham.

Nelly found that there was a good deal to be done to the grenadine dress when she looked it over critically, and became very diligent. It was quiet in and about the house for a long time, until suddenly she heard the sound of heavy footsteps coming in from the road. The side-door was in a little entry between the room where Nelly sat and the kitchen, and the new-comer knocked loudly. "A tramp," said Nelly to herself; while Melissa came to open the door, wiping her hands hurriedly on her apron.

"I wonder if you couldn't give me something to eat," said the man.

"I suppose I could," answered Melissa. "Will you step in?" Beggars were very few in Longfield, and Miss Dane never wished anybody to go away hungry from her house. It was off the grand highway of tramps; but they were by no means unknown.

Melissa searched among her stores, and

Nelly heard her putting one plate after another on the kitchen table, and thought that the breakfast promised to be a good one, if it were late.

"Don't put yourself out," said the man, as he moved his chair nearer. "I lodged in an old barn three or four miles above here last night, and there did n't seem to be very good board there."

"Going far?" inquired Melissa concisely.

"Boston," said the man. "I 'm a little too old to travel afoot. Now if I could go by water, it would seem nearer. I 'm more used to the water. This is a royal good piece o' beef. I suppose you could n't put your hand on a mug of cider?" This was said humbly; but the tone failed to touch Melissa's heart.

"No, I could n't," said she decisively; so there was an end of that, and the conversation flagged for a time.

Presently Melissa came to speak to Miss Dane, who had just come downstairs. "Could you stay in the kitchen a few minutes?" she whispered. "There 's an old creatur' there that looks foreign. He came to the door for something to eat, and I gave it to him; but he 's miser'ble looking, and I

don't like to leave him alone. I'm just in
the midst o' dressing the chickens. He'll
be through pretty quick, according to the
way he's eating now."

Miss Dane followed her without a word;
and the man half rose, and said, "Good-
morning, madam!" with unusual courtesy.
And, when Melissa was out of hearing, he
spoke again: "I suppose you haven't any
cider?" to which his hostess answered, "I
could n't give you any this morning," in a
tone that left no room for argument. He
looked as if he had had a great deal too
much to drink already.

"How far do you call it from here to
Boston?" he asked, and was told that it was
eighty miles.

"I'm a slow traveler," said he; "sailors
don't take much to walking." Miss Dane
asked him if he had been a sailor. "Nothing else," replied the man, who seemed much
inclined to talk. He had been eating like a
hungry dog, as if he were half-starved, — a
slouching, red-faced, untidy-looking old man,
with some traces of former good looks still
to be discovered in his face. "Nothing else.
I ran away to sea when I was a boy, and I
followed it until I got so old they would n't

ship me even for cook." There was something in his feeling, for once, so comfortable, — perhaps it was being with a lady like Miss Dane, who pitied him, — that lifted his thoughts a little from their usual low level. "It's drink that's been the ruin of me," said he. "I ought to have been somebody. I was nobody's fool when I was young. I got to be mate of a firstrate ship, and there was some talk o' my being captain before long. She was lost that voyage, and three of us were all that was saved; we got picked up by a Chinese junk. She had the plague aboard of her, and my mates died of it, and I was down myself. It was a hell of a place to be in. When I got ashore I shipped on an old bark that pretended to be coming round the Cape, and she turned out to be a pirate. I just went to the dogs, and I've gone from bad to worse ever since."

"It's never too late to mend," said Melissa, who came into the kitchen just then for a string to tie the chickens.

"Lord help us, yes, it is!" said the sailor. "It's easy for you to say that. I'm too old. I ain't been master of this craft for a good while." And he laughed at his melancholy joke.

" Don't say that," said Miss Dane.

" Well, now, what could an old wrack like me do to earn a living? and who 'd want me if I could? You would n't. I don't know when I 've been treated so decent as this before. I 'm all broke down." But his tone was no longer sincere; he had fallen back on his profession of beggar.

" Could n't you get into some asylum or — there 's the Sailors' Snug Harbor, is n't that for men like you? It seems such a pity for a man of your years to be homeless and a wanderer. Have n't you any friends at all?" And here, suddenly, Miss Dane's face altered, and she grew very white; something startled her. She looked as one might who saw a fearful ghost.

" No," said the man; " but my folks used to be some of the best in Salem. I have n't shown my head there this good while. I was an orphan. My grandmother brought me up. You see, I did n't come back to the States for thirty or forty years. Along at the first of it I used to see men in port that I used to know; but I always dodged 'em, and I was way off in outlandish places. I 've got an awful sight to answer for. I used to have a good wife when I was in Australia.

I don't know where I have n't been, first and last. I was always a gay fellow. I 've spent as much as a couple o' fortunes, and here I am a-begging. Devil take it ! "

Nelly was still sewing in the dining-room ; but, soon after Miss Dane had gone out to the kitchen, one of the doors between had slowly closed itself with a plaintive whine. The round stone which Melissa used to keep it open had been pushed away. Nelly was a little annoyed ; she liked to hear what was going on ; but she was just then holding her work with great care in a place that was hard to sew, so she did not move. She heard the murmur of voices, and thought, after a while, that the old vagabond ought to go away by this time. What could be making her cousin Horatia talk so long with him ? It was not like her at all. He would beg for money, of course, and she hoped Miss Horatia would not give him a single cent.

It was some time before the kitchen-door opened, and the man came out with clumsy, stumbling steps. " I 'm much obliged to you," he said, " and I don't know but it is the last time I 'll get treated as if I was a gentleman. Is there anything I could do for you round the place?" he asked hesitatingly. and as if he hoped that his offer would not be accepted.

"No," answered Miss Dane. "No, thank you. Good-by!" and he went away.

The old beggar had been lifted a little above his low life; he fell back again directly before he was out of the gate. "I'm blessed if she didn't give me a ten-dollar bill!" said he. "She must have thought it was one. I'll get out o' call as quick as I can; hope she won't find it out, and send anybody after me." Visions of unlimited drinks, and other things in which it was possible to find pleasure, flitted through his stupid mind. "How the old lady stared at me once!" he thought. "Wonder if she was anybody I used to know? 'Downton?' I don't know as I ever heard of the place." And he scuffed along the dusty road; and that night he was very drunk, and the next day he went wandering on, God only knows where.

But Nelly and Melissa both heard a strange noise in the kitchen, as if some one had fallen, and they found that Miss Horatia had fainted dead away. It was partly the heat, she said, when she saw their anxious faces as she came to herself; she had had a little headache all the morning; it was very hot and close in the kitchen, and the faintness had come upon her suddenly. They helped her to walk into the cool parlor presently, and Melissa brought her a glass of wine, and Nelly sat beside her on a footstool as she lay on the sofa, and fanned her. Once she held her cheek against Miss Horatia's hand for a minute, and she will never know as long as she lives, what a comfort she was that day.

Every one but Miss Dane forgot the old sailor tramp in this excitement that followed his visit. Do you guess already who he was? But the certainty could not come to you with the chill and horror it did to Miss Dane. There had been something familiar in his look and voice from the first, and then she had suddenly known him, her lost lover. It was an awful change that the years had made in him. He had truly called himself a wreck; he was like some dreary wreck in its decay and utter ruin, its miserable ugliness and worthlessness, falling to pieces in the slow tides of a lifeless southern sea.

And he had once been her lover, Miss Dane thought bitterly, many times in the days that followed. Not that there was ever

anything asked or promised between them,
but they had liked each other dearly, and
had parted with deep sorrow. She had
thought of him all these years so tenderly ;
she had believed always that his love had
been even greater than her own, and never
once had doubted that the missing brig
Chevalier had carried with it down into the
sea a heart that was true to her.

By little and little this all grew familiar,
and she accustomed herself to the knowledge
of her new secret. She shuddered at the
thought of the misery of a life with him, and
she thanked God for sparing her such shame
and despair. The distance between them
seemed immense. She had always been a
person of so much consequence among her
friends, and so dutiful and irreproachable a
woman. She had not begun to understand
what dishonor is in the world ; her life had
been shut in by safe and orderly surroundings. It was a strange chance that had
brought this wanderer to her door. She remembered his wretched untidiness. She
had not liked even to stand near him. She
had never imagined him grown old : he had
always been young to her. It was a great
mercy he had not known her ; it would

have been a most miserable position for them both; and yet she thought, with sad surprise, that she had not known she had changed so entirely. She thought of the different ways their roads in life had gone; she pitied him; she cried about him more than once; and she wished that she could know he was dead. He might have been such a brave, good man, with his strong will and resolute courage. God forgive him for the wickedness which his strength had been made to serve! "God forgive him!" said Miss Horatia to herself sadly over and over again. She wondered if she ought to have let him go away, and so have lost sight of him; but she could not do anything else. She suffered terribly on his account; she had a pity, such as God's pity must be, for even his willful sins.

So her romance was all over with; yet the townspeople still whispered it to strangers, and even Melissa and Nelly never knew how she had really lost her lover in so strange and sad a way in her latest years. Nobody noticed much change; but Melissa saw that the whale's tooth disappeared from its place in Miss Horatia's room, and her old friends said to each other that she began to show her age a great deal. She seemed really like an old woman now; she was not the woman she had been a year ago.

This is all of the story; but we so often wish, when a story comes to an end, that we knew what became of the people afterward. Shall we believe that Miss Horatia clings more and more fondly to her young cousin Nelly; and that Nelly will stay with her a great deal before she marries, and sometimes afterward, when the lieutenant goes away to sea? Shall we say that Miss Dane seems as well satisfied and comfortable as ever, though she acknowledges she is not so young as she used to be, and secretly misses something out of her life? It is the contentment of winter rather than that of summer: the flowers are out of bloom for her now, and under the snow. And Melissa, will not she always be the same, with a quaintness and freshness and toughness like a cedar-tree, to the end of her days? Let us hope they will live on together and be untroubled this long time yet, the two good women; and let us wish Nelly much pleasure, and a sweet soberness and fearlessness as she grows older and finds life a harder thing to understand, and a graver thing to know.

THE COURTING OF SISTER WISBY.

ALL the morning there had been an increasing temptation to take an out - door holiday, and early in the afternoon the temptation outgrew my power of resistance. A far-away pasture on the long southwestern slope of a high hill was persistently present to my mind, yet there seemed to be no particular reason why I should think of it. I was not sure that I wanted anything from the pasture, and there was no sign, except the temptation, that the pasture wanted anything of me. But I was on the farther side of as many as three fences before I stopped to think again where I was going, and why.

There is no use in trying to tell another person about that afternoon unless he distinctly remembers weather exactly like it. No number of details concerning an Arctic ice-blockade will give a single shiver to a child of the tropics. This was one of those perfect New England days in late summer, when the spirit of autumn takes a first stealthy flight, like a spy, through the ripening country - side, and, with feigned sympathy for those who droop with August heat, puts her cool cloak of bracing air about leaf and flower and human shoulders. Every living thing grows suddenly cheerful and strong; it is only when you catch sight of a horror-stricken little maple in swampy soil, — a little maple that has second sight and foreknowledge of coming disaster to her race, — only then does a distrust of autumn's friendliness dim your joyful satisfaction.

In midwinter there is always a day when one has the first foretaste of spring; in late August there is a morning when the air is for the first time autumn like. Perhaps it is a hint to the squirrels to get in their first supplies for the winter hoards, or a reminder that summer will soon end, and everybody had better make the most of it. We are always looking forward to the passing and ending of winter, but when summer is here it seems as if summer must always last. As I went across the fields that day, I found myself half lamenting that the world must fade again, even that the best of her budding and bloom was only a preparation for another spring-time, for an awakening beyond the coming winter's sleep.

The sun was slightly veiled; there was a chattering group of birds, which had gathered for a conference about their early migration. Yet, oddly enough, I heard the voice of a belated bobolink, and presently saw him rise from the grass and hover leisurely, while he sang a brief tune. He was much behind time if he were still a housekeeper; but as for the other birds, who listened, they cared only for their own notes. An old crow went sagging by, and gave a croak at his despised neighbor, just as a black reviewer croaked at Keats: so hard it is to be just to one's contemporaries. The bobolink was indeed singing out of season, and it was impossible to say whether he really belonged most to this summer or to the next. He might have been delayed on his northward journey; at any rate, he had a light heart now, to judge from his song, and I wished that I could ask him a few questions, — how he liked being the last man among the bobolinks, and where he had taken singing lessons in the South.

Presently I left the lower fields, and took a path that led higher, where I could look beyond the village to the northern country mountainward. Here the sweet fern grew, thick and fragrant, and I also found myself heedlessly treading on pennyroyal. Near by, in a field corner, I long ago made a most comfortable seat by putting a stray piece of board and bit of rail across the angle of the fences. I have spent many a delightful hour there, in the shade and shelter of a young pitch-pine and a wild-cherry tree, with a lovely outlook toward the village, just far enough away beyond the green slopes and tall elms of the lower meadows. But that day I still had the feeling of being outward bound, and did not turn aside nor linger. The high pasture land grew more and more enticing.

I stopped to pick some blackberries that twinkled at me like beads among their dry vines, and two or three yellow-birds fluttered up from the leaves of a thistle, and then came back again, as if they had complacently discovered that I was only an overgrown yellow-bird, in strange disguise but perfectly harmless. They made me feel as if I were an intruder, though they did not offer to

peck at me, and we parted company very
soon. It was good to stand at last on the
great shoulder of the hill. The wind was
coming in from the sea, there was a fine fragrance from the pines, and the air grew
sweeter every moment. I took new pleasure
in the thought that in a piece of wild pasture
land like this one may get closest to Nature,
and subsist upon what she gives of her own
free will. There have been no drudging,
heavy-shod ploughmen to overturn the soil,
and vex it into yielding artificial crops.
Here one has to take just what Nature is
pleased to give, whether one is a yellow-bird
or a human being. It is very good entertainment for a summer wayfarer, and I am asking my reader now to share the winter provision which I harvested that day. Let us
hope that the small birds are also faring
well after their fashion, but I give them an
anxious thought while the snow goes hurrying in long waves across the buried fields,
this windy winter night.

I next went farther down the hill, and
got a drink of fresh cool water from the
brook, and pulled a tender sheaf of sweet
flag beside it. The mossy old fence just beyond was the last barrier between me and

the pasture which had sent an invisible messenger earlier in the day, but I saw that
somebody else had come first to the rendezvous : there was a brown gingham cape-
bonnet and a sprigged shoulder-shawl bob-
bing up and down, a little way off among
the junipers. I had taken such uncommon
pleasure in being alone that I instantly felt
a sense of disappointment ; then a warm
glow of pleasant satisfaction rebuked-my self-
ishness. This could be no one but dear old
Mrs. Goodsoe, the friend of my childhood
and fond dependence of my maturer years.
I had not seen her for many weeks, but here
she was, out on one of her famous campaigns
for herbs, or perhaps just returning from a
blueberrying expedition. I approached with
care, so as not to startle the gingham bonnet ; but she heard the rustle of the bushes
against my dress, and looked up quickly, as
she knelt, bending over the turf. In that
position she was hardly taller than the luxuriant junipers themselves.

" I 'm a-gittin' in my mulleins," she said
briskly, " an' I 've been thinking o' you
these twenty times since I come out o' the
house. I begun to believe you must ha'
forgot me at last."

"I have been away from home," I explained. "Why don't you get in your
pennyroyal too? There's a great plantation
of it beyond the next fence but one."

"Pennyr'yal!" repeated the dear little
old woman, with an air of compassion for
inferior knowledge; "'t ain't the right time,
darlin'. Pennyr'yal's too rank now. But
for mulleins this day is prime. I've got a
dreadful graspin' fit for 'em this year; seems
if I must be goin' to need 'em extry. I feel
like the squirrels must when they know a
hard winter's comin'." And Mrs. Goodsoe
bent over her work again, while I stood by
and watched her carefully cut the best full-
grown leaves with a clumsy pair of scissors,
which might have served through at least
half a century of herb-gathering. They
were fastened to her apron-strings by a long
piece of list.

"I'm going to take my jack-knife and
help you," I suggested, with some fear of re-
fusal. "I just passed a flourishing family
of six·or seven heads that must have been
growing on purpose for you."

"Now be keerful, dear heart," was the
anxious response; "choose 'em well.
There's odds in mulleins same's there is in

angels. Take a plant that's all run up to
stalk, and there ain't but little goodness in
the leaves. This one I'm at now must ha'
been stepped on by some creatur' and
blighted of its bloom, and the leaves is han'-
some! When I was small I used to have a
notion that Adam an' Eve must a took mulleins fer their winter wear. Ain't they just
like flannel, for all the world? I've had experience, and I know there's plenty of sickness might be saved to folks if they'd quit
horse-radish and such fiery, exasperating
things, and use mullein drarves in proper
season. Now I shall spread these an' dry
'em nice on my spare floor in the garrit, an'
come to steam 'em for use along in the
winter there'll be the vally of the whole
summer's goodness in 'em, sartin." And
she snipped away with the dull scissors,
while I listened respectfully, and took great
pains to have my part of the harvest present
a good appearance.

"This is most too dry a head," she added
presently, a little out of breath. "There!
I can tell you there's win'rows o' young
doctors, bilin' over with book-larnin', that
is truly ignorant of what to do for the sick,
or how to p'int out those paths that well

people foller toward sickness. Book-fools I call 'em, them young men, an' some on 'em never 'll live to know much better, if they git to be Methuselahs. In my time every middle-aged woman, who had brought up a family, had some proper ideas o' dealin' with complaints. I won't say but there was some fools amongst *them*, but I 'd rather take my chances, unless they 'd forsook herbs and gone to dealin' with patent stuff. Now my mother really did sense the use of herbs and roots. I never see anybody that come up to her. She was a meek-looking woman, but very understandin', mother was."

"Then that 's where you learned so much yourself, Mrs. Goodsoe," I ventured to say.

"Bless your heart, I don't hold a candle to her; 't is but little I can recall of what she used to say. No, her l'arnin' died with her," said my friend, in a self-depreciating tone. "Why, there was as many as twenty kinds of roots alone that she used to keep by her, that I forget the use of; an' I 'm sure I should n't know where to find the most of 'em, any. There was an herb" — *airb*, she called it — "an herb called master-wort, that she used to get way from Pennsylvany; and she used to think everything

of noble-liverwort, but I never could seem
to get the right effects from it as she could.
Though I don't know as she ever really did
use masterwort where somethin' else wouldn't
a served. She had a cousin married out in
Pennsylvany that used to take pains to get
it to her every year or two, and so she felt
't was important to have it. Some set more
by such things as come from a distance, but
I rec'lect mother always used to maintain
that folks was meant to be doctored with
the stuff that grew right about 'em; 't was
sufficient, an' so ordered. That was before
the whole population took to livin' on wheels,
the way they do now. 'T was never my
idee that we was meant to know what 's
goin' on all over the world to once. There 's
goin' to be some sort of a set-back one o'
these days, with these telegraphs an' things,
an' letters comin' every hand's turn, and
folks leavin' their proper work to answer
'em. I may not live to see it. 'T was allowed to be difficult for folks to git about
in old times, or to git word across the country, and they stood in their lot an' place,
and weren't all just alike, either, same as
pine-spills."

We were kneeling side by side now, as if

in penitence for the march of progress, but we laughed as we turned to look at each other.

"Do you think it did much good when everybody brewed a cracked quart mug of herb-tea?" I asked, walking away on my knees to a new mullein.

"I've always lifted my voice against the practice, far's I could," declared Mrs. Goodsoe; "an' I won't deal out none o' the herbs I save for no such nonsense. There was three houses along our road, — I call no names, — where you could n't go into the livin' room without findin' a mess o' herb-tea drorin' on the stove or side o' the fireplace, winter or summer, sick, or well. One was thoroughwut, one would be camomile, and the other, like as not, yellow dock; but they all used to put in a little new rum to git out the goodness, or keep it from spilin'." (Mrs. Goodsoe favored me with a knowing smile.) "Land, how mother used to laugh! But, poor creaturs, they had to work hard, and I guess it never done 'em a mite o' harm; they was all good herbs. I wish you could hear the quawkin' there used to be when they was indulged with a real case o' sickness. Everybody would collect from

far an' near; you 'd see 'em coming along
the road and across the pastures then; everybody clamorin' that nothin' would n't do no
kind o' good but her choice o' teas or drarves
to the feet. I wonder there was a babe
lived to grow up in the whole lower part o'
the town; an' if nothin' else 'peared to ail
'em, word was passed about that 't was likely
Mis' So-and-So's last young one was goin'
to be foolish. Land, how they 'd gather!
I know one day the doctor come to Widder
Peck's and the house was crammed so 't he
could scercely git inside the door; and he
says, just as polite, ' Do send for some of
the neighbors! ' as if there wa'n't a soul to
turn to, right or left. You 'd ought to seen
'em begin to scatter."

"But don't you think the cars and telegraphs have given people more to interest
them, Mrs. Goodsoe? Don't you believe
people's lives were narrower then, and more
taken up with little things?" I asked, un-
wisely, being a product of modern times.

"Not one mite, dear," said my companion
stoutly. "There was as big thoughts then
as there is now; these times was born o'
them. The difference is in folks themselves;
but now, instead o' doin' their own house-

keepin' and watchin' their own neighbors, — though that was carried to excess, — they git word that a niece's child is ailin' the other side o' Massachusetts, and they drop everything and git on their best clothes, and off they jiggit in the cars. 'T is a bad sign when folks wears out their best clothes faster 'n they do their every-day ones. The other side o' Massachusetts has got to look after itself by rights. An' besides that, Sunday-keepin' 's all gone out o' fashion. Some lays it to one thing an' some another, but some o' them old ministers that folks are all a-sighin' for did preach a lot o' stuff that wa'n't nothin' but chaff; 't wa'n't the word o' God out o' either Old Testament or New. But everybody went to meetin' and heard it, and come home, and was set to fightin' with their next door neighbor over it. Now I 'm a believer, and I try to live a Christian life, but I 'd as soon hear a surveyor's book read out, figgers an' all, as try to get any simple truth out o' most sermons. It 's them as is most to blame."

"What was the matter that day at Widow Peck's?" I hastened to ask, for I knew by experience that the good, clear-minded soul beside me was apt to grow unduly vexed and

distressed when she contemplated the state
of religious teaching.

"Why, there wa'n't nothin' the matter,
only a gal o' Miss Peck's had met with a
dis'pintment and had gone into screechin'
fits. 'T was a rovin' creatur' that had come
along hayin' time, and he'd gone off an'
forsook her betwixt two days; nobody ever
knew what become of him. Them Pecks
was 'Good Lord, anybody!' kind o' gals,
and took up with whoever they could get.
One of 'em married Heron, the Irishman;
they lived in that little house that was burnt
this summer, over on the edge o' the plains.
He was a good-hearted creatur', with a
laughin' eye and a clever word for everybody.
He was the first Irishman that ever came
this way, and we was all for gettin' a look at
him, when he first used to go by. Mother's
folks was what they call Scotch-Irish, though;
there was an old race of 'em settled about
here. They could foretell events, some on 'em,
and had the second sight. I know folks used
to say mother's grandmother had them gifts,
but mother was never free to speak about
it to us. She remembered her well, too."

"I suppose that you mean old Jim Heron,
who was such a famous fiddler?" I asked

with great interest, for I am always delighted
to know more about that rustic hero, paro-
chial Orpheus that he must have been !

" Now, dear heart, I suppose you don't remember him, do you ? " replied Mrs. Goodsoe,
earnestly. " Fiddle ! He 'd about break
your heart with them tunes of his, or else set
your heels flying up the floor in a jig, though
you was minister o' the First Parish and all
wound up for a funeral prayer. I tell ye
there ain't no tunes sounds like them used
to. It used to seem to me summer nights
when I was comin' along the plains road,
and he set by the window playin', as if there
was a bewitched human creatur' in that old
red fiddle o' his. He could make it sound
just like a woman's voice tellin' somethin'
over and over, as if folks could help her out
o' her sorrows if she could only make 'em
understand. I 've set by the stone-wall and
cried as if my heart was broke, and dear
knows it wa'n't in them days. How he would
twirl off them jigs and dance tunes ! He
used to make somethin' han'some out of 'em
in fall an' winter, playin' at huskins and
dancin' parties; but he was unstiddy by
spells, as he got along in years, and never
knew what it was to be forehanded. Every-

body felt bad when he died; you could n't help likin' the creatur'. He 'd got the gift — that 's all you could say about it.

"There was a Mis' Jerry Foss, that lived over by the brook bridge, on the plains road, that had lost her husband early, and was left with three child'n. She set the world by 'em, and was a real pleasant, ambitious little woman, and was workin' on as best she could with that little farm, when there come a rage o' scarlet fever, and her boy and two girls was swept off and laid dead within the same week. Every one o' the neighbors did what they could, but she 'd had no sleep since they was taken sick, and after the funeral she set there just like a piece o' marble, and would only shake her head when you spoke to her. They all thought her reason would go; and 't would certain, if she could n't have shed tears. An' one o' the neighbors — 't was like mother's sense, but it might have been somebody else —spoke o' Jim Heron. Mother an' one or two o' the women that knew her best was in the house with her. 'T was right in the edge o' the woods and some of us younger ones was over by the wall on the other side of the road where there was a couple of old willows, — I remember just how the brook damp felt; and we kept quiet 's we could, and some other folks come along down the road, and stood waitin' on the little bridge, hopin' somebody 'd come out, I suppose, and they 'd git news. Everybody was wrought up, and felt a good deal for her, you know. By an' by Jim Heron come stealin' right out o' the shadows an' set down on the doorstep, an' 't was a good while before we heard a sound; then, oh, dear me! 't was what the whole neighborhood felt for that mother all spoke in the notes, an' they told me afterwards that Mis' Foss's face changed in a minute, and she come right over an' got into my mother's lap, — she was a little woman, — an' laid her head down, and there she cried herself into a blessed sleep. After awhile one o' the other women stole out an' told the folks, and we all went home. He only played that one tune.

"But there!" resumed Mrs. Goodsoe, after a silence, during which my eyes were filled with tears. "His wife always complained that the fiddle made her nervous. She never 'peared to think nothin' o' poor Heron after she 'd once got him."

"That 's often the way," said I, with harsh cynicism, though I had no guilty person in

my mind at the moment; and we went straying off, not very far apart, up through the
pasture. Mrs. Goodsoe cautioned me that
we must not get so far off that we could not
get back the same day. The sunshine began
to feel very hot on our backs, and we both
turned toward the shade. We had already
collected a large bundle of mullein leaves,
which were carefully laid into a clean, calico
apron, held together by the four corners, and
proudly carried by me, though my companion regarded them with anxious eyes. We
sat down together at the edge of the pine
woods, and Mrs. Goodsoe proceeded to fan
herself with her limp cape-bonnet.

"I declare, how hot it is! The east wind's
all gone again," she said. "It felt so cool
this forenoon that I overburdened myself
with as thick a petticoat as any I've got. I'm
despri't afeared of having a chill, now that I
ain't so young as once. I hate to be housed
up."

"It's only August, after all," I assured
her unnecessarily, confirming my statement
by taking two peaches out of my pocket, and
laying them side by side on the brown pine
needles between us.

"Dear sakes alive!" exclaimed the old

lady, with evident pleasure. "Where did you get them, now? Does n't anything taste twice better out-o'-doors? I ain't had such a peach for years. Do le's keep the stones, an' I 'll plant 'em; it only takes four year for a peach pit to come to bearing, an' I guess I 'm good for four year, 'thout I meet with some accident."

I could not help agreeing, or taking a fond look at the thin little figure, and her wrinkled brown face and kind, twinkling eyes. She looked as if she had properly dried herself, by mistake, with some of her mullein leaves, and was likely to keep her goodness, and to last the longer in consequence. There never was a truer, simple-hearted soul made out of the old-fashioned country dust than Mrs. Goodsoe. I thought, as I looked away from her across the wide country, that nobody was left in any of the farm-houses so original, so full of rural wisdom and reminiscence, so really able and dependable, as she. And nobody had made better use of her time in a world foolish enough to sometimes undervalue medicinal herbs.

When we had eaten our peaches we still sat under the pines, and I was not without pride when I had poked about in the ground

with a little twig, and displayed to my
crony a long fine root, bright yellow to the
eye, and a wholesome bitter to the taste.

" Yis, dear, goldthread," she assented in-
dulgently. " Seems to me there's more of
it than anything except grass an' hardhack.
Good for canker, but no better than two or
three other things I can call to mind; but I
always lay in a good wisp of it, for old
times' sake. Now, I want to know why you
should a bit it, and took away all the taste
o' your nice peach? I was just thinkin'
what a han'some entertainment we've had.
I 've got so I 'sociate certain things with
certain folks, and goldthread was somethin'
Lizy Wisby could n't keep house without,
no ways whatever. I believe she took so
much it kind o' puckered her disposition."

" Lizy Wisby? " I repeated inquiringly.

" You knew her, if ever, by the name of
Mis' Deacon Brimblecom," answered my
friend, as if this were only a brief preface
to further information, so I waited with
respectful expectation. Mrs. Goodsoe had
grown tired out in the sun, and a good story
would be an excuse for sufficient rest. It
was a most lovely place where we sat, half-
way up the long hillside; for my part, I was

perfectly contented and happy. " You 've often heard of Deacon Brimblecom ? " she asked, as if a great deal depended upon his being properly introduced.

" I remember him," said I. "They called him Deacon Brimfull, you know, and he used to go about with a witch-hazel branch to show people where to dig wells."

" That 's the one," said Mrs. Goodsoe, laughing. " I did n't know 's you could go so far back. I 'm always divided between whether you can remember everything I can, or are only a babe in arms."

" I have a dim recollection of there being something strange about their marriage," I suggested, after a pause, which began to appear dangerous. I was so much afraid the subject would be changed.

" I can tell you all about it," I was quickly answered. " Deacon Brimblecom was very pious accordin' to his lights in his early years. He lived way back in the country then, and there come a rovin' preacher along, and set everybody up that way all by the ears. I 've heard the old folks talk it over, but I forget most of his doctrine, except some of his followers was persuaded they could dwell among the an-

gels while yet on airth, and this Deacon
Brimfull, as you call him, felt sure he was
called by the voice of a spirit bride. So
he left a good, deservin' wife he had, an'
four children, and built him a new house
over to the other side of the land he'd had
from his father. They did n't take much
pains with the buildin', because they expected to be translated before long, and
then the spirit brides and them folks was
goin' to appear and divide up the airth
amongst 'em, and the world's folks and on-
believers was goin' to serve 'em or be sent
to torments. They had meetins about in
the school-houses, an' all sorts o' goins on ;
some on 'em went crazy, but the deacon held
on to what wits he had, an' by an' by the
spirit bride did n't turn out to be much of
a housekeeper, an' he had always been used
to good livin', so he sneaked home ag'in.
One o' mother's sisters married up to Ash
Hill, where it all took place ; that's how I
come to have the particulars."

"Then how did he come to find his Eliza
Wisby ?" I inquired. "Do tell me the
whole story ; you've got mullein leaves
enough."

"There's all yesterday's at home, if I

have n't," replied Mrs. Goodsoe. "The way he come a-courtin' o' Sister Wisby was this: she went a-courtin' o' him.

"There was a spell he lived to home, and then his poor wife died, and he had a spirit bride in good earnest, an' the child'n was placed about with his folks and hers, for they was both out o' good families; and I don't know what come over him, but he had another pious fit that looked for all the world like the real thing. He had n't no family cares, and he lived with his brother's folks, and turned his land in with theirs. He used to travel to every meetin' an' conference that was within reach of his old sorrel hoss's feeble legs; he j'ined the Christian Baptists that was just in their early prime, and he was a great exhorter, and got to be called deacon, though I guess he wa'n't deacon, 'less it was for a spare hand when deacon timber was scercer 'n usual. An' one time there was a four days' protracted meetin' to the church in the lower part of the town. 'T was a real solemn time; something more 'n usual was goin' forward, an' they collected from the whole country round. Women folks liked it, an' the men too; it give 'em a change, an' they was quartered

round free, same as conference folks now.
Some on 'em, for a joke, sent Silas Brimblecom up to Lizy Wisby's, though she'd
give out she could n't accommodate nobody,
because of expectin' her cousin's folks.
Everybody knew 't was a lie; she was
amazin' close considerin' she had plenty to
do with. There was a streak that wa'n't
just right somewheres in Lizy's wits, I always thought. She was very kind in case o'
sickness, I 'll say that for her.

"You know where the house is, over there
on what they call Windy Hill? There the
deacon went, all unsuspectin', and 'stead o'
Lizy 's resentin' of him she put in her own
hoss, and they come back together to evenin'
meetin'. She was prominent among the
sect herself, an' he bawled and talked, and
she bawled and talked, an' took up more 'n
the time allotted in the exercises, just as if
they was showin' off to each other what they
was able to do at expoundin'. Everybody
was laughin' at 'em after the meetin' broke
up, and that next day an' the next, an' all
through, they was constant, and seemed to
be havin' a beautiful occasion. Lizy had
always give out she scorned the men, but
when she got a chance at a particular one

't was altogether different, and the deacon seemed to please her somehow or 'nother, and — There! you don't want to listen to this old stuff that 's past an' gone?"

"Oh yes, I do," said I.

" I run on like a clock that 's onset her striking hand," said Mrs. Goodsoe mildly. " Sometimes my kitchen timepiece goes on half the forenoon, and I says to myself the day before yisterday I would let it be a warnin', and keep it in mind for a check on my own speech. The next news that was heard was that the deacon an' Lizy — well, opinions differed which of 'em had spoke first, but them fools settled it before the protracted meetin' was over, and give away their hearts before he started for home. They considered 't would be wise, though, considerin' their short acquaintance, to take one another on trial a spell; 't was Lizy's notion, and she asked him why he would n't come over and stop with her till spring, and then, if they both continued to like, they could git married any time 't was convenient. Lizy, she come and talked it over with mother, and mother disliked to offend her, but she spoke pretty plain; and Lizy felt hurt, an' thought they was showin' excellent judgment, so much harm come from hasty unions and folks comin' to a realizin' sense of each other's failin's when 't was too late.

"So one day our folks saw Deacon Brimfull a-ridin' by with a gre't coopful of hens in the back o' his wagon, and bundles o' stuff tied on top and hitched to the exes underneath; and he riz a hymn just as he passed the house, and was speedin' the old sorrel with a willer switch. 'T was most Thanksgivin' time, an' sooner 'n she expected him. New Year's was the time she set; but he thought he'd better come while the roads was fit for wheels. They was out to meetin' together Thanksgivin' Day, an' that used to be a gre't season for marryin'; so the young folks nudged each other, and some on' 'em ventured to speak to the couple as they come down the aisle. Lizy carried it off real well; she wa'n't afraid o' what nobody said or thought, and so home they went. They 'd got out her yaller sleigh and her hoss; she never would ride after the deacon's poor old creatur', and I believe it died long o' the winter from stiffenin' up.

"Yes," said Mrs. Goodsoe emphatically, after we had silently considered the situation for a short space of time, — "yes, there

was consider'ble talk, now I tell you! The
raskil boys pestered 'em just about to death
for a while. They used to collect up there
an' rap on the winders, and they 'd turn out
all the deacon's hens 'long at nine o'clock
'o night, and chase 'em all over the dingle;
an' one night they even lugged the pig right
out o' the sty, and shoved it into the back
entry, an' run for their lives. They 'd stuffed
its mouth full o' somethin', so it could n't
squeal till it got there. There wa'n't a
sign o' nobody to be seen when Lizy hasted
out with the light, and she an' the deacon
had to persuade the creatur' back as best
they could; 't was a cold night, and they
said it took 'em till towards mornin'. You
see the deacon was just the kind of a man
that a hog would n't budge for; it takes a
masterful man to deal with a hog. Well,
there was no end to the works nor the talk,
but Lizy left 'em pretty much alone. She
did 'pear kind of dignified about it, I must
say!"

"And then, were they married in the
spring?"

"I was tryin' to remember whether it was
just before Fast Day or just after," responded my friend, with a careful look at

the sun, which was nearer the west than
either of us had noticed. " I think likely
't was along in the last o' April, any way
some of us looked out o' the window one
Monday mornin' early, and says, ' For goodness' sake! Lizy 's sent the deacon home
again !' His old sorrel havin' passed away,
he was ridin' in Ezry Welsh's hoss-cart,
with his hen-coop and more bundles than
he had when he come, and he looked as
meechin' as ever you see. Ezry was drivin',
and he let a glance fly swiftly round to see
if any of us was lookin' out; an' then I
declare if he did n't have the malice to turn
right in towards the barn, where he see my
oldest brother, Joshuay, an' says he real natural, ' Joshuay, just step out with your
wrench. I believe I hear my kingbolt rat-
tlin' kind o' loose.' Brother, he went out
an' took in the sitooation, an' the deacon
bowed kind of stiff. Joshuay was so full o'
laugh, and Ezry Welsh, that they could n't
look one another in the face. There wa'n't
nothing ailed the kingbolt, you know, an'
when Josh riz up he says, ' Goin' up country for a spell, Mr. Brimblecom ?'

" ' I be,' says the deacon, lookin' dreadful
mortified and cast down.

"'Ain't things turned out well with you an' Sister Wisby?' says Joshuay. 'You had ought to remember that the woman is the weaker vessel.'

"'Hang her, let her carry less sail, then!' the deacon bu'st out, and he stood right up an' shook his fist there by the hen-coop, he was so mad; an' Ezry's hoss was a young creatur', an' started up an set the deacon right over backwards into the chips. We did n't know but he 'd broke his neck; but when he see the women folks runnin' out, he jumped up quick as a cat, an' clim' into the cart, an' off they went. Ezry said he told him that he could n't git along with Lizy, she was so fractious in thundery weather; if there was a rumble in the day-time she must go right to bed an' screech, and if 't was night she must git right up an' go an' call him out of a sound sleep. But everybody knew he 'd never a gone home unless she 'd sent him.

"Somehow they made it up agin right away, him an' Lizy, and she had him back. She 'd been countin' all along on not havin' to hire nobody to work about the gardin an' so on, an' she said she wa'n't goin' to let him have a whole winter's board for nothin'. So the old hens was moved back, and they was married right off fair an' square, an' I don't know but they got along well as most folks. He brought his youngest girl down to live with 'em after a while, an' she was a real treasure to Lizy; everybody spoke well o' Phebe Brimblecom. The deacon got over his pious fit, and there was consider'ble work in him if you kept right after him. He was an amazin' cider-drinker, and he airnt the name you know him by in his latter days. Lizy never trusted him with nothin', but she kep' him well. She left everything she owned to Phebe, when she died, 'cept somethin' to satisfy the law. There, they're all gone now: seems to me sometimes, when I get thinkin,' as if I 'd lived a thousand years!"

I laughed, but I found that Mrs. Goodsoe's thoughts had taken a serious turn.

"There, I come by some old graves down here in the lower edge of the pasture," she said as we rose to go. "I could n't help thinking how I should like to be laid right out in the pasture ground, when my time comes; it looked sort o' comfortable, and I have ranged these slopes so many summers. Seems as if I could see right up through the turf and tell when the weather was pleasant, and get the goodness o' the sweet fern. Now, dear, just hand me my apernful o' mulleins out o' the shade. I hope you won't come to need none this winter, but I 'll dry some special for you."

" I 'm going home by the road," said I, " or else by the path across the meadows, so I will walk as far as the house with you. Are n't you pleased with my company?" for she demurred at my going the least bit out of the way.

So we strolled toward the little gray house, with our plunder of mullein leaves slung on a stick which we carried between us. Of course I went in to make a call, as if I had not seen my hostess before; she is the last maker of muster-gingerbread, and before I came away I was kindly measured for a pair of mittens.

" You 'll be sure to come an' see them two peach-trees after I get 'em well growin'?" Mrs. Goodsoe called after me when I had said good-by, and was almost out of hearing down the road.